MAKER

DOVE SEASON

ROBIN BRANDE

RYER PUBLISHING

MAKER
(Dove Season)
By Robin Brande

Published by Ryer Publishing
www.ryerpublishing.com

www.robinbrande.com
"Time Map" was published in *Pulphouse* Magazine Issue #20
www.pulphousemagazine.com
Cover art by Andrey Strelkov/Deposit Photos
Cover design by Ryer Publishing

Print ISBN: 978-1-952383-44-1
Ebook ISBN: 978-1-952383-45-8

ALSO BY ROBIN BRANDE

<u>Dove Season Universe</u>

Dove Season

Finder

Seeker

Believer

Maker

Explorer

<u>Winnie Parsons Mysteries</u>

The Genius Track

A Man of Appetites

A Drop of Sweat

The Long Gray Hook

The Slip of a Rib

<u>Parallelogram Quartet</u>

Into the Parallel

Caught in the Parallel

Seize the Parallel

Beyond the Parallel

<u>Young Adult</u>

Evolution, Me & Other Freaks of Nature

Fat Cat

Doggirl

Replay

<u>Bradamante Saga</u>

Book of Earth

Book of Water

<u>Romance</u>

Love Proof

Freefall

Heart of Ice

Fire and Ice

<u>Collections</u>

The Love of a Good Dog

Mountain Tough

The Miraculous Unknown

<u>Self-Help</u>

What If You're Doing It Right?

What If You're Doing It Right? For Teens

CONTENTS

DOVE SEASON UNIVERSE
RECOMMENDED READING ORDER

MAKER

TIME MAP

TIME MAP

The handcuff on my right wrist was much tighter than it needed to be. I wasn't going anywhere. But I understood their need to assert some authority. The whole base was on high alert.

They had lost three priceless *assets*, as the people interrogating me kept calling them. I never corrected them. What would be the point? They didn't want my opinion, they didn't want my enlightened world view, they only wanted to know how I helped their assets escape. Right under their noses. No security cam footage, no clues, nothing.

They had me in one of the small concrete interview rooms, one-way mirror, just like in a TV cop show. The other half of the handcuff was attached to the leg of a gray metal table that was bolted into the floor.

I'd already been held for about three or four hours. There was no clock in the room, they took my watch, but you get a sense of blocks of time. They let me have one bathroom break, escorted by a guard, then back to the hard metal chair to wait and wait.

I was still in my blue coveralls and black work boots. No one took my shoelaces, so I guess they weren't worried I'd try to hang myself. From what? The table leg? I knew they were watching me through the glass. I just sat and thought my thoughts.

Mostly about how slick it all was. None of it my idea, which made it all the better. I could just shake my head at it and go along and watch the show unfold.

Plus I learned a lot in that last critical hour. Things I certainly never knew and didn't even suspect.

In the almost seven years I'd been there, you could say I befriended the guys. The *assets*. They were easy to like.

But before I got the job, I had to go through two weeks of psychological testing. I figured working as a civilian for the military, there would be all sorts of hurdles, but the psych questions were strange.

They showed me all sorts of pictures and videos of men, women, boys, and girls, all of every possible nationality and color.

They had me hooked up to sensors to see if I reacted negatively at all. Of course I didn't. I'm a black man, I've spent my life with prejudice, so you think I care if someone is Pakistani or Chinese or Native American? Come one, come all, I'll judge you by your actions. If you're an ass, you're an ass, I don't care what color you are. But if you're good people, then fine. Come sit by me.

And then, week two, they started slipping in some new

kinds of pictures. People with horrible disfigurements. People who had obviously survived being burned. People who might have made a living with a traveling circus back in the old days, the only way they could support themselves.

And then, aliens. Cartoon aliens at first, little green Martians, then little gray extraterrestrials from science fiction movies.

Any reaction, Mr. Swan?

They checked my readouts. Didn't matter to me, green, gray, disfigured, any of it. I'd lived a life. I'd seen a lot of people.

Just to make sure I wasn't totally dead, they also showed me scenes from horror movies where face-eating aliens were stalking normal folk. I didn't care for those, because who would? They checked my readouts. Elevated heart rate, fast breathing, I guess they liked what they saw.

Because I got the job. Technician Specialist. Top security clearance.

I know I came highly recommended. My old boss at Champion Rigs must have known someone in the Army, because they came looking for me, not the other way around. I didn't know their secret base in the wilderness outside Aspen, Colorado even existed.

The rules were strict. You live on base. You don't leave. You don't travel. We provide everything you need for free: food, comfortable housing, clothing, medical care, transportation, you name it.

I was recently out of a marriage and without a lot of personal prospects. I figured I'd take the job for a year or two, just to get my feet back under me. And learn some new things.

I've been what people call a mechanical wizard ever since I was a little boy. Not just normal fix-it and build-it kind of childhood play, but next level. When I was five I took apart my mother's vacuum and a few other appliances around the house, and used the parts to make a working spaceship for my plastic army men. I got it airborne. I've always been a nut about flight.

Teachers noticed me, they put me in programs. I won all sorts of competitions. Reggie Swan became a name. My picture in the paper, holding up those big fake checks that show thousands of dollars in prize money—that was me. I made a good living as a kid.

And just like basketball and football standouts who start getting scouted while they're still in junior high, my parents started getting offers early on. Scholarships to this college or that. High-paying tech jobs with Boeing and Ford and a lot of other companies. And military recruiters telling them why I'd do best in the Army, Air Force, or whoever that particular recruiter represented.

But I have a stubborn streak in me. A real obsession with not being bossed around. And I had a different plan in mind.

Learn everything. Try everything. Not the college route, that wasn't for me, but hands-on. Working cars and airplanes and ships for a while. Then bridges and high rises. Whatever someone could design and build, I wanted to have my hands on that. Learn how everything worked, down to the nuts and bolts and motors and rivets.

If you start at sixteen, like I did, you can work a lot of jobs by the time you're forty-six.

But I parked myself at Base X for six years and ten months—the longest I stayed anywhere—because there was more to learn there than anyplace else. I would have stayed there for the rest of my life if I could have kept learning from the guys.

When I finally got clearance to begin the job, the supervisor, Greg, took me to a special room for my orientation.

It was a little bigger than the one where they held me after they arrested me, but it had the same light gray concrete walls and metal table and metal chairs.

Greg said, "They tell me your psych eval was clean. But I won't let you on the floor until I know you can handle it."

I had no idea what he was talking about. All they told me was I'd be working on high-tech flight simulators and maybe some special aircraft. It sounded interesting, but not something anyone would have to *handle.*

The door opened, a woman stepped through, and after her came three little kids.

I thought they were kids. But only for a half a second. Then the light in my brain went on...

Whoa.

They were about three feet tall. Hairless. Skin a pale pinkish-gray. Heads more of an oval shape than round.

Their eyes were gentle and beautiful. That was the first thing I thought. It took me a moment to realize how much larger than were than a human's. Maybe three times as large, and oval, and lidless. But the way they looked into my eyes, I just loved them right away.

I know that sounds strange for a grown man to say about extraterrestrials, but the bond was immediate. Like bonding with an animal just from the way it looks into your eyes.

You just *know.* You may be different species, but you are the same. You belong. The trust and the bond are real.

I smiled. I think I even laughed. But with a kind of wild joy that I got to see three such extraordinary beings.

My new supervisor was watching me closely all the time. He seemed relieved at my reaction.

I found out later there had been two other tech specialists before me who washed out the first time they met their new coworkers. Both of them freaked out so mightily, doctors had to come in and give them sedatives.

Then the techs were whisked off the base under all sort of security. I have no idea what happened to them after that.

Because they were risks now to the secret program on the base. They had seen and they couldn't unsee. They couldn't be allowed to talk about it, ever. The military has experience dealing with things like that.

But I wasn't going to be a problem. I was all in, from minute one.

The woman who had escorted the three extraterrestrials into the room introduced them as RJ, LX, and MT.

No kinds of names for friends. I renamed them RayJay, Linus, and Mit.

And finally I found out why I was there.

The three extraterrestrials—ETs, for easier reference— hadn't been captured, like I read might have happened back in the 1940s when spaceships started getting shot down in places like Roswell, New Mexico.

These three ETs had shown up on Base X voluntarily one day. Just out of the blue. I found out from talking to some of the officers that there have been all sorts of spaceships over the years hovering around military complexes, especially ones with nuclear weapons.

Like they're monitoring us. Trying to make sure these Neanderthals aren't blowing up their world like foolish teenagers playing around with gasoline and matches.

But RayJay and Linus and Mit didn't just buzz the base or disable the missiles, like some other ETs have done at other military installations. Instead, they came straight in one day, flying a disk-shaped craft with a glowing blue dome on top, and they landed on the airstrip right where any gawking personnel could see.

Communication was a challenge. It took a while to find someone suitable to act as interpreter.

It took a week, in fact, before they somehow found Kirsten Simmens, the woman who escorted them into the room the day I first met them.

She was an attractive young woman in her late twenties when I first met her, small, slender, with pale skin and long blonde hair. I don't know where they found her or how. There must be some kind of database, though, because her skills were perfectly suited to this case.

RayJay and the other two had small slits for mouths, but they didn't seem to have the mechanism for speech. No vocal cords. Nothing that allowed them to make any noise at all. I never heard them groan or laugh or cry. It would have been like trying to communicate with a fish.

They spoke with their eyes. They latched on with their gaze and you just knew what they were feeling. Sad, scared, frustrated, delighted—I felt many of their emotions over the years.

But Kirsten Simmens could do more than just feel what they felt. She could hear what they wanted to tell her.

It was at a particular frequency, she explained to me when she realized I was ready to learn how to do it myself. Like tuning in to a faint and secret radio station that you could only access if the ETs gave you a special dial.

Not everyone could hear them, even if they wanted to. RayJay and Linus and Mit were in charge. They decided who could hear them and couldn't.

And then when you did hear them—it made me laugh the first time. Because they were mimics. They talked to you in your own voice.

"Hey, Reggie?"

"Yeah, Reggie?"

That's what it sounded like. Like me having a conversation with myself in my own head.

Kirsten spent a lot of time with the three ETs and gained their trust. And the fact was, they wanted to be able to talk to someone. They had come to this planet and this particular base on purpose. It was no accident.

But they were new to the planet, obviously, and didn't know which humans they should trust with their knowledge.

I came along two months after they'd already been there.

And I don't think it's an exaggeration to say I became their best friend.

They showed me. They taught me. They confided in me. Not just the mechanics of their spaceship that they intended to give to us humans.

They told me everything I asked. About themselves, about their people, about the planet that they came from, and their galaxy. All of it.

And they taught me how to build a spaceship like theirs. They taught me things maybe no other ET has shared with any other humans.

I learned how to easily create anti-gravity propulsion. How to make a ship invisible. How to pilot one without installing any levers or controls, but only by thinking to it with my mind.

RayJay told me he hadn't planned on sharing those extra details. He had specific instructions about how much to teach the Earthlings. He and the others were here to help us advance, as others like them had come before—many times over the millennia—but they were supposed to dole out just so much at a time. To keep our more primitive minds from overloading. And also to make sure we were using their technology for good, not to invent new ways of killing ourselves. We already had enough of those.

But RayJay could see that I was different. I could understand as much as he decided to teach me. And my heart is peaceful. I'm not a man of violence.

And RayJay knew that I loved him and Linus and Mit.

He knew I would always protect them, I would never betray them, I only wanted what was best for them all the time.

I gave up caring about any of my old life. About anything outside the base. I didn't need anything but to work and to learn morning until night.

I would take the eleven o'clock bus back to my housing on base every night just so I could shower and sleep for a few hours, then I'd come right back on the first bus at six.

And I'd been living that way, loving every minute of my life, for the past almost seven years. My brain felt like it had grown ten times bigger than it ever was. I had learned so much about the universe and space travel and other life forms, I could write a hundred books on them to start and still have more to say.

But even the best things can't last. Think of your favorite dog or cat, dying too soon, when you wish they would live with you your whole life.

You still have all that love for them, you would still want them by your side even when you're an old, old man, but that isn't how life works. Even extraterrestrial life.

I could see that RayJay wasn't looking right for a while. His skin was losing the pink tint that always made all three of them look like they were blushing.

He was getting to be a duller and duller gray.

Finally I said, "RayJay, are you dying on me?"

He answered me in my own voice, speaking directly into my head. "Reggie, we have to go soon. Will you help us?"

We were alone in the special hangar where they kept

the guys' ship. Only a few personnel were allowed to come in there.

So we were alone at the moment, just the four of us, and I bawled like a baby. I couldn't make myself stop.

I hugged RayJay. Then the other two guys came in for the hug, too, and we stood there, just clinging to each other like brothers who were about to be separated.

They didn't make any noise, but I could hear them inside my mind crying with the same sound I was making. Like hearing myself, and then three echoes of the same sobs. It made it so much worse to know that they were feeling it, too.

But then I got hold of myself. I said of course I'll help you however I can.

And then RayJay let me in on yet another secret. Of how I could help them escape.

I asked them to wait one more day. I wasn't ready to say goodbye. But I understood that RayJay needed to go back or he wasn't going to make it.

They told me they knew from the start that they would only stay for seven years. They had prepared their bodies to survive in our atmosphere for that long.

And they knew that I would be with them for almost all of those seven years.

"How did you know?"

"We saw you," came my own voice in my head. "On our time map."

They had hinted about their time map a few times before, but I never really understood what they meant.

"Do you mean time travel?" I asked them the first time,

but they said it wasn't exactly that. "Is it a time machine?" I tried. "You see a time on your map and you can go there?"

But still the answer was no.

Now RayJay tried one more time to help me understand. He pressed one of his four pale gray fingers into his chest where a heart would be if he was a human instead of what he was.

Then he drew a line through the space between us, and pressed that same finger to where he knew my heart was.

"Beginning," said the Reggie voice in my mind, "end. Time to end of time."

"But you saw it," I said, trying to grasp what he meant. "Like looking at a map, but not of a place. It was of a time."

I could feel RayJay smiling with his eyes. And I heard the rest of his explanation, and finally understood.

Before coming to Earth with Linus and Mit, they had looked at a time map to see when to come.

Just as they had consulted other maps to find the best location to bring their gift of technology to teach the humans. And just as other extraterrestrials before them had chosen the best time to bring their own earlier technology to humans living in earlier times.

Why are there suddenly a rash of discoveries and advances in different places around the world, all in the same few years?

Because the leaders of the ETs send out teams. They try to seed our planet with knowledge by sharing information with people they think can understand it. Little by little, bringing us children along. Helping us to do better. Helping us to understand the better and peaceful ways so maybe some day in the future we can join the greater unified community and not just try to shoot everybody who looks and sounds different.

So RayJay and the other two volunteered to be one of the teams. And they knew they had seven years to do as much as they could for as long as their bodies could survive. But which seven years should they use?

They saw me on their time map. Reginald Swan, making my way through a life as best as I could.

Not knowing I would get the job Base X. Not even dreaming I would one day meet RayJay and Linus and Mit.

But they knew. They saw it. Just like astronomers can map out the future paths of the stars.

So they landed when they did, and they waited for someone like Kirsten to come along to explain why they were here and what they intended to do.

And then they waited longer still, just a few more months, for their friend to show up, answering a job offer that didn't exist before they arrived.

I passed the psych test. I would accept people of all kind. I would accept aliens. I wouldn't freak out.

To the contrary, the minute I saw those three, it was like I'd come home to a planet I didn't know I had left.

And then all my lifelong mechanical wizardry finally had a reason to be.

If they had time, I wish they could have shown me how to make a time map of my own. To find out what to do next, now that they were leaving.

But there wasn't time. I could see that. RayJay had waited as long as he safely could.

Linus and Mit were still looking healthy to my eyes, but I knew they would soon look as gray and sickly as RayJay.

You have to let people go. Even if you don't want to. And I was ready to do whatever I could to help them.

So they gave me the one more day that I asked for, and they told me as much as they could about whatever else I wanted to know.

Including how to help them escape. It took so little effort. That's why it worked so well.

They did not travel through the stars to get here to Earth. They didn't travel light years. They didn't travel distance.

They traveled time and dimension. Both of them entangled together. They slipped from their time and dimension into ours.

To our human sensibilities, they must have needed a spaceship to do it. And I spent the last seven years picking it apart and reverse-engineering it and learning about anti-gravity and all of its other special properties.

When they never needed the ship at all. And they proved it to me when they left.

They asked me to bring three items from my home. Small metal objects that were easy to conceal.

I plucked out three clean teaspoons from my kitchen drawer their last morning. And even though I was sad, desperately sad to know my friends were leaving, I still had to smile to myself at the absurdity of thinking these spoons were somehow going to transport them to a galaxy so far away.

I knew that whatever they were going to show me

would be the last perfect lesson. But I couldn't even guess how it was all going to work out.

I dressed in my blue coveralls and heavy black work boots. I stuck the three spoons in my coveralls pocket.

I took the six o'clock bus. I didn't even pause at the commissary for my usual cup of coffee. I was too sad and nervous. I wanted both to delay it and to get it over with.

The three of them were waiting for me in the hangar beside their ship. The security cameras that monitored us at all times would have seen us greet each other and go inside the ship as we did almost every day.

There were no cameras inside the ship. There wasn't room and there wasn't a place to mount them. The interior walls were curved and smooth and there was barely space for the three small extraterrestrials and one six-foot human.

I had to lie on my back, scrunched behind their command seats. But I loved it inside their ship and never minded the discomfort.

The walls always glowed with a faint kind of golden color, not metallic, but more like the first glow of sunrise.

It was always the perfect temperature, even though the hangar was too freezing in the winter and way too sweltering in the summer. Inside the craft it was always just right.

In the closed-in space I could smell the unique scent of the ETs. Both earthy and lemony. Like citrus-scented soil. I always wondered if they minded the way I smelled so sweaty at the end of a day. It was why I always wanted to shower at least once a day, to try to make it a little nicer for them.

But they never seemed offended by all the human aspects of me. They never minded any of my human failings.

My impatience when I wasn't learning as fast as I wanted, or when I couldn't easily understand what they were trying to say.

My anger sometimes at the way things were run on the base. The way people sometimes treated me like an underling to be bossed around.

My awkward, gangly physical form that couldn't copy their elegant motions with even a fraction of their finesse. Their ship was a work of art. Sometimes I felt like a gorilla trying to mimic the delicate work of their hands.

They forgave me all my failings. They embraced me as their brother.

And now it was time to say goodbye. I didn't even try to hold back my tears.

I pulled out the teaspoons from my pocket and gave them to RayJay. He handed one each to Linus and Mit.

Then RayJay struck his spoon against the smooth golden wall of his ship. I could hear a faint tinkling, like a vibrating chime.

Linus and Mit struck their spoons against the wall, too, and RayJay said this was a resonance. The sound and vibration were all they needed.

I looked into their eyes. I could feel the love they felt for me. I know they could feel my love for them.

Then with the sound of three goodbyes in my head, all

of them in my own voice, my teachers slipped away, like disappearing behind a hidden wall. One moment they were there, and the next the spoons fell with a ting to the floor of their craft and my three dearest friends were gone back to their homes.

I stayed there for a while. I couldn't bring myself to move. I cried like a boy who had just had to put down his beloved dog.

But I couldn't hide inside that spacecraft for very long. I had promised the guys I would cover their trail.

So I pulled myself together. I slapped my palms against my cheeks. I took some deep breaths. I had to do this right.

I climbed out of the craft like I'd done a hundred times before. No big deal, the ETs were obviously still inside working on something.

I went to the commissary and got myself a coffee and a danish. I made myself sit at one of the tables and take my time eating.

I went back to the hangar, knowing there were cameras that could confirm everything I did. I waved to where the guys would have been sitting inside their ship, and motioned that I just had to go do something first, and I'd be right back.

All to stretch out the time. All to confuse anyone who might try to piece together what had really happened.

Not that they could. I could barely understand it myself. But I promised the guys I would protect them all the way to the end.

I fiddled around at my locker for a little while, then I returned to the hangar and got ready to do the big act.

I climbed up to the ship and called out for RayJay. I opened it and looked inside.

Then I looked around the hangar and called to RayJay again.

I pretended to be puzzled. I started asking around. You seen the guys? Where could they be?

And then I saw Kirsten Simmens with her long blonde hair running through the door of the hangar, looking panicked.

She lived on the base, just like me, there to help facilitate communication with the ETs if anyone needed it. I don't know what she did most of the day, since I had no trouble talking to the guys myself and I never saw anyone else trying to talk to them separately.

Most everyone was afraid. They kept away. That was fine with RayJay and the guys. They had been told to be wary of most humans, and to try to find just a few who would understand them and want to help them, like Kirsten Simmens and me.

"Where are they?" Kirsten called to me. "They're not here!"

How she knew, I wasn't really sure.

She must have been locked onto their frequency even when she wasn't directly communicating with them. But whatever it was, she knew they were gone.

And then everybody knew. Kirsten made sure of that. I don't blame her, she was honestly upset.

And in time, just like I knew they would, the powers that be decided I had done something bad.

Four MPs showed up, ready to try to wrestle me to the

ground. I held up my hands to show them I'd come willingly.

But they still cuffed my wrists before taking me on the perp walk across the base. And then they cuffed me to the heavy metal table in the interrogation room.

And for four hours I answered the same damn questions, posed by a parade of different people in charge: *What did you do with them? Where did you hide them?*

And then at some point they must have realized the ETs weren't hiding anywhere on base. Maybe because Kirsten Simmens said she couldn't sense them.

So then the questions were about how I helped them escape.

What could I say? That I gave them three spoons and *poof*? I said I had no idea where the guys were now. No reason to believe they escaped. They liked it here. Didn't we all treat them well? Why would they leave?

But no one seemed to be buying it. I was in trouble. Even though no one could prove I had any part of it. But I was the last one to see them, and that always means something.

So I sat there locked to the table and wondered how it was all going to sort out.

They took me to a cell eventually to sleep out the night. I lay on the hard bunk and stared up at the gray concrete ceiling.

I tried to imagine where RayJay and the guys were now. What they were doing. Where they lived. Who their people were.

How happy they all must have been to return to their

home world. Even explorers eventually long for something familiar. Their favorite foods, their favorite places, the faces of people they love.

I wondered where I would go now. If I would ever return to my old life. Or if I was going to get disappeared like the two techs who washed out before me.

Or was I about to spend the rest of my life in some military prison?

If I had a time map of my own, I might have been able to see it.

But I guess smarter minds realized what they had in me. A man full of information and knowledge that shouldn't go to waste.

Locking me up in prison wouldn't help them create supertech spaceships of their own. What do we do with Reggie Swan? I became just another asset.

On my second day of interrogation I waited chained to the same gray metal table. I had a few bathroom breaks, escorted by a guard.

And then some time in the afternoon the door to the room opened again, and someone new came in, accompanied by Kirsten Simmens.

The man was shorter than me, maybe five-six, but buff and stocky, like he had been a wrestler back in his youth.

He was in his thirties, I guessed, white with brown hair and brown eyes. He wore a button-down shirt and a dark blue tie.

No jacket, so I could see the sweat stains in his pits. Maybe he had traveled all night to get to me and didn't have time to change his clothes.

He smiled at me and held out his hand. "Ted Whitling, Mr. Swan. Nice to meet you."

Kirsten took a seat and Whitling took the other. The three of us sat for a moment just judging what to do.

Kirsten had taught me where to find the right frequency to talk to the guys. But what I didn't realize was she and I could keep talking there even after they were gone.

I heard her in my head, talking in her own voice, not mine.

"He's from the government. One of their intelligence agencies. He's the one who found me and brought me here seven years ago. I think we can trust him."

"I don't trust anyone right now," I thought back to Kirsten. *"He's going to have to prove it."*

And it went on like that, with Ted Whitling talking to me out loud and Kirsten and I talking to each other in secret.

Whitling was different from the others. He didn't ask me any questions. Instead he spent his time telling me what he could do for me.

"I think you need to face something," he said. "This is the end of the road here." He looked at Kirsten. "For both of you. If you want to keep going, you have to pick a new road."

I wasn't sure what he meant by *keep going.* Was he telling us the military might decide to kill us for what we knew?

I had heard things. I wasn't happy to think it might happen to me, but I can't say I was surprised.

Or was Whitling just giving Kirsten Simmens and me career counseling? Telling us we were in dead-end jobs now and we needed to level up?

"Doing what?" I asked him. "What's the new road?"

Ted Whitling smiled. "I'd rather not discuss it here."

We were being watched and no doubt recorded. Whitling wasn't stupid. But neither am I, and I needed more than a vague promise.

Kirsten was young, but she had obviously learned a few things, too. She told me, *"We need some guarantee of our safety."*

"So, are we assets now, too?" I asked Whitling. "Are we being traded to someone else? Is that it, our lives aren't our own anymore?"

Whitling smiled. "Look, Mr. Swan. I'm going to be honest. I'm just a cog in a big machine, the same as you and Ms. Simmens. We aren't special. I'm afraid we can all be replaced. They just remove the defective part and stick another one in."

"I'm just a cog," I repeated.

"That's right," Whitling said. "So let's be smart about where we put you next."

Kirsten and I looked at each other.

I could see she didn't believe it any more than I did.

Not special? The hell with that. Kirsten Simmens and I were bright, shiny special if there ever was one. Both of us had just spent seven years getting to know three extraterrestrials. We couldn't just be plucked out and replaced by anyone else.

I don't know what RayJay and the others told Kirsten

over that time, but they had sure filled my brain with exactly the kind of valuable information any government would want.

So I wasn't buying this idea that we were just replaceable cogs in a machine.

And it was time to make a deal that I wanted.

I have never been motivated by money or power. Those don't interest me in the least.

But everybody has their price.

All I've ever wanted since I was a little boy was to learn everything. Try everything. Know everything that there was to know.

What Ted Whitling should have said was the road stops here, and from now on you're cut off and you'll never learn the rest.

But I could see that on my own. And that was what I didn't want to lose. I wanted to take what RayJay, Linus, and Mit had taught me, and then keep going and going from there.

I couldn't speak for Kirsten Simmens, but if Whitling could find me a new place to slip in as a cog in the big machine, then as long as I could keep learning more, my answer was going to be yes.

But mindful of Kirsten, I said, "How are you going to guarantee our safety?"

"I'd like to discuss that with you," he said, "but not here."

I looked at Kirsten. She was chewing the side of her thumbnail. But her mind was working, too, even though she wasn't talking to me through all of the steps.

Maybe she, too, had no interest in returning to whatever her life had been before. How much work was there for extraterrestrial translators out in the regular world?

So both of us took Whitling's offer, not really knowing what it all meant.

But it was enough to know that he got them to take the handcuff off me right away. And that he and Kirsten and I would be leaving Base X on a jet within the hour.

I didn't bother going back to my place. I never really lived there, I lived for my work.

But Kirsten quickly packed a small bag and joined us as fast as she could.

Even though she still asked me, *"Do you think they're going to dispose of us?"*

I didn't think so, but how could I be sure?

But once we were in the air, jetting away from the base, Whitling took off his tie and visibly relaxed.

"Will you tell me how they did it?" he asked me. "How they got away?"

I thought about it, and told him maybe later, when I got to know him better.

If he wanted that from me, it was some leverage. I wasn't about to throw it away.

But the time came when I did tell him. That and a whole lot more.

It's been ten years now. Ten astonishing years. Years when I've gotten to make the most out of everything RayJay and the guys taught me.

All I can say is that I made the right choice. I can't speak for Kirsten, but she seems to be doing all right. They've even trained her to do more than just sit on the sidelines and wait for some extraterrestrials to show up needing a translator.

She goes out and finds them. She listens to the frequency in her head, and she knows where to go to greet them and show them to safety.

I told her that was what RayJay tried to teach me. About their time maps that told the extraterrestrials when to come.

How he drew a line from where his heart would have been if he were human, and drew it across the space between us to where my heart was.

I took it to mean he could feel me. Across the distances between our galaxies, on this planet where he intended to land.

He adjusted his travel for when he knew I would be here, ready to befriend him and learn everything he wanted to teach me.

"Maybe all of them have time maps," I told Kirsten. "And maybe the dot on some of their maps is *you*."

She's not the only one. There are people like Kirsten roaming all over the world right now, waiting to greet the teams that are coming to teach us.

"If you see RayJay," I told her. "Or Linus, or Mit…"

She gripped my arm and gave me a smile.

But I'm not counting on them coming back. They never said that they would.

Instead they taught me how to go and find them.

I've been working ten years on transportation of my own. Not only building ships for the *machine*, as Ted Whitling called it, but also building one for me.

It's exactly like RayJay's, with smooth, curved walls inside that seem to glow golden like the first rays of sunrise.

The walls make a particular sound when you strike them with an ordinary metal teaspoon—one of the three that I saved from where they fell after the guys went away that day. Their spoons still vibrate at a particular frequency.

I've done tests. I've gone on short excursions.

And now it's time to go further afield.

But it isn't just the resonance or the sound or the vibration that take you there. It's also the time map you hold in your heart.

You reach out to someone on the other end. And when you find them, you lock on to the path you need to take.

Heart to heart across the galaxies. Back to the planet where you belong. At exactly the right time, so they're waiting for you there.

Tomorrow I'm leaving to go find my friends.

They're a dot on a time map, and my heart knows where to find them.

LINGUIST

LINGUIST

People think they understand telepathy. At least conceptually. Not how to do it, but what it is.

They think it's mind to mind, a sender and a receiver. One person sending a piece of information, and the other person catching it out of the air somehow. I've even heard of people practicing it like a bingo game: C7. Right. C7. Message received.

It is not that way at all.

Telepathy isn't mind to mind, it's mind to *information.*

I used to describe it as swimming out in the ocean of all knowledge and scooping out a cupful and looking at it closely, tasting the saltiness of it, hearing the wind and waves all around you, feeling the force of the sea and letting it carry you as far as you want to go.

But that's just for the lay people. It's not the truth. I've never thought anyone who can't do it would understand.

But you've asked me. Persistently. And you seem like

you have at least some basic knowledge. More than the average person.

So I'll tell you, but if it doesn't resonate, then I can't help you more than this.

TED WHITLING: Thank you. Mind if I start the recording?

KIRSTEN SIMMENS: Uh, no. I guess not.

TED WHITLING: Just take your time. We'll take as long as you need.

KIRSTEN SIMMENS: Okay. Thank you.

I have had this skill, this talent for as long as I can remember.

TED WHITLING: How old are you?

KIRSTEN SIMMENS: Thirty-four. I was born in Cicero, New York to two engineers. You would think math would be my skill.

But math is too dry. It feels dead to my mind. Numbers and symbols, as dusty as chalk, as cold as icy feet.

But *language*. Cuddle up with it. Build a fire. Put a blanket around you. Drink hot chocolate with a mile-high tower of whipped cream on top.

I've had a few boyfriends over the years, and no one would call them lookers, but damn, those boys could *talk*.

Digress. Sorry, I'm a little nervous. I don't usually talk about this stuff.

TED WHITLING: It's okay. Take your time.

KIRSTEN SIMMENS: My parents are lovely, practical people. John and Jeannie. They met at work, had the same sense of humor, and they're still a great match. They've been very accepting of me, not rigid. I'm sure that's made all the difference.

After she had me, my mother took a few years off to stay at home. I'm sure some people can't remember anything from when they were that little, but I at least remember the feeling. I loved it. My mother is very playful. So when it first happened, she thought I was just doing make-believe like we always did.

She was cooking something on the stove and I was sitting at the kitchen table coloring in my coloring book. My mom saved the picture. It was an elephant I was sure should be purple.

I started talking to myself in some kind of gibberish. I'd say a few words, click my tongue, say some more, click, talk.

My mom listened while I carried on a whole conversation and kept coloring with my purple crayon.

I've watched videos of young twins talking to each other in their secret language, and from what I understand, I sounded like that. Like I was sure I was using real words. I was very serious about it.

Finally my mother decided to join the game. "Who are you talking to?" she asked.

I gave her some name I can't remember, but it sounded like nonsense to her.

"Is that your friend?" my mother asked.

"No," I told her. "I don't know him, but he's lost and he asked me for help."

I'm sure my mother laughed. But she loved me and

always indulged me. "Maybe I can help," she said. "I'm good with maps. Where is he trying to go?"

I said another gibberish word full of consonants and vowels and clicks.

"I don't know that place," she said.

"Okay." I continued coloring my purple elephant, but my mother could see that I was upset. I can imagine it. I hate to disappoint people. I hate to see anyone hurt. If someone was lost and needed my help, even at three years old I would have felt responsible.

A moment later I set down my crayon and looked at my mother with tearful eyes. "Can we *try?*"

"Of course, sweetie. Come on, let's go look at the globe."

There was a spinning globe on a stand in my playroom. My engineer parents were always very conscious of trying to raise me right. They talked to me like a real person, not a baby. They took my childish questions seriously and answered them as best they could.

"Where is he trying to go?" my mother asked.

I repeated the question in my clicks and gibberish. And I listened.

I pointed to a spot in South Africa.

Then I drew a line with my finger from the globe into the air, about two inches above it. "Here, but he isn't sure how far it is. He was supposed to meet the rest of his family."

"Here, in the air," my mother said.

I nodded. "He's a spaceman. He's lost. He wants to go home."

I have no idea how my mother talked me out of my

concern. I'm sure when she told my father about it later, the two of them must have thought it was adorable. But it was nothing to worry about. All little children have imaginary playmates.

A few weeks later, my mother and I were out for a walk in our neighborhood. I had a new doll, Molly, and she came with a doll-sized stroller I loved to push up and down our sidewalk.

A few doors down from us lived Mr. and Mrs. Virtanen, an elderly couple who always made a fuss over me. Mr. Virtanen was out in front of his house watering his bushes. He paused to come admire my stroller and my doll.

I have no memory of him, but I've seen a picture. He was short and a little pudgy and had a very sweet face and a welcoming smile.

"Is this your new dolly?" he asked.

"Yes." Then I introduced her in Finnish. And I continued speaking Finnish to Mr. Virtanen, much to his utter astonishment.

It was his native language. How on earth did I know? How could I speak it so fluently? He asked me questions in Finnish and I answered. I'm sure it was effortless on my part.

My mother must have stood there in frozen shock. And probably fear, even though she never told me she felt that way.

But how could she not? Her dear little girl was an absolute freak.

To hear my parents tell it, that's when they realized I had a special talent with languages.

A special talent would have meant hearing it or reading it and somehow picking it up very quickly.

But I was the one who initiated the conversation. Mr. Virtanen never spoke a word of Finnish to me before that.

My mother didn't even know he and his wife were from Finland. It was all a surprise to her.

I could count off a hundred stories just like this. The Serbian woman I went up to in a grocery store when I was four. I took her hand and started speaking to her in her own language because I could sense she was feeling afraid. She needed to use the restroom, but she had no idea where to go or who to ask. She didn't speak English and her brother who did was off in another aisle.

No problem. A blonde-haired four-year-old girl in pink shorts and a pink top and pink flip-flops was here to save the day. I took her by the hand and walked her to where my mother had taken me to the bathroom in the grocery store before.

I forgot to tell my father, who had brought me shopping with him that day, that I was leaving. When he turned around in the produce section and realized I was missing, he panicked. Of course he would. He ran from aisle to aisle, frantically searching for me. He finally saw me walking back, holding the hand of the grateful Serbian lady as I escorted her back to the produce section where I had found her.

So, the question is—the question has always been—how do I know? How do I guess people's languages, and more important, how I do I understand languages I've never heard or spoken before?

Because I do understand them. I can speak fluently any language from any country.

All I have to do is put myself in the way of what I have come to think of as a wave of words. It's not the way I've told it before, like floating on the ocean of knowledge and dipping my cup into it and drawing it out.

It's more like a vibrating field I can feel as soon as I step inside it. I can almost feel it tickling against my skin. I can decide to keep on walking through it and ignore what I hear, or I can stand still and let the field embrace me. I can choose to absorb it while I'm there and bathe in whatever language I'm hearing and feel that same language come rolling off my tongue. I can feel it spreading out and relaxing inside my mind.

This is my form of telepathy. I am open to this specific kind of information. I have never had to study any language before I'm able to understand it or speak it.

I can't, just to be clear, sit down and write it. I've tried that. My talent doesn't extend that far. I've looked at phrases in Spanish, Italian, Finnish, Serbian, and thousands of other languages I know I've spoken. But the written words look completely foreign to me. I can't even pronounce any of the words phonetically.

But I can hear the words and understand them, and I can hold full conversations in that same language. And not just basic vocabulary. Full, fluent discussions like I've been speaking it my whole life.

TED WHITLING: Including alien languages.

KIRSTEN SIMMENS: Yes. So we're going there? Yes. I

mean, you know that, but … okay, I mean I'm sure it's in my file, right? I've been doing it for the past seven years.

TED WHITLING: How did the Army find you?

KIRSTEN SIMMENS: Army Intelligence, if that makes a difference. I had applied to work at the United Nations as an interpreter. Seems like the right fit, right? I double-majored in French and German in college, then got my Masters in both of them too, just to have something. I thought maybe I'd teach some day. I honestly had no idea what to do with my life. Or with my talent. Not that I told anyone about it. All my instructors just thought I was extraordinarily good at picking it all up. Eventually one of them pointed me toward the UN. She had some connection there.

So I went to the interview, and … well, you probably know this part.

TED WHITLING: Maybe not. Tell me.

KIRSTEN SIMMENS: It's … it's kind of embarrassing. One of the interviewers was this fat old man who just instantly got the hairs on my arms standing up. The way he was leering at me. Not even trying to hide it.

TED WHITLING: General Kosta.

KIRSTEN SIMMENS: Then you do know.

TED WHITLING: I'd like to hear it from your perspective.

KIRSTEN SIMMENS: I don't know why he was there. Maybe they always include someone from a military branch. Maybe he was just bored and looking for something to do. But I started hearing him. In my head.

Speaking—no, not speaking, *thinking*—in Greek. Imagining … me. Things he'd like to do to me. It's not something I like to remember. Can we move on?

TED WHITLING: Tell me what happened.

KIRSTEN SIMMENS: I'm sure I got all red in the face, and even though I'm normally very respectful of authority, something got into me. It was just so … extremely disgusting. I stood up, there in my proper little suit and high heels and looking like the least dangerous person you can imagine, and I let him *have* it. I started shouting at him in Greek, using as much filthy language as he was thinking about me, and it was like a street scene, I was gesticulating and practically spitting at him and telling him what kind of a pig he was and how dare he—it probably went on for a good three or four minutes. I was … I guess what set me off was it was the first time I'd ever heard something like that. All women can tell when someone is undressing them in their minds, but I'd never had to hear it before. Ever. It was a real shock to my system. To have that invade my mind. Not pleasant at all.

Plus, really, how dare he. Someone's grandfather, he was that old. And he's thinking such disgusting thoughts about me? I was like a child in comparison. Pervert. I just wasn't having it. I don't know how else to explain it.

TED WHITLING: What happened?

KIRSTEN SIMMENS: Interview suspended, obviously. There were three women in the room, and even though none of them probably understood Greek, they knew exactly what I was yelling about. All women know.

The senior one, Claire McGivens, I'm sure you've heard of her—

TED WHITLING: Yes.

KIRSTEN SIMMENS: She threw the General out. And asked me to stay. I was still on my feet, still hot as a cannon, but once they got that pervert out, I calmed down fairly quickly.

She apologized. Again, very little question what went on. But at the same time, a little surprising that no one was saying, *But how did you know?* They all took it in stride.

Ms. McGivens asked me if that happens to me often.

I said no, that was the first time.

She said, "You read his mind?"

I had to think quickly. Should I lie? But all three women were looking at me as if they already knew it was obvious.

So I nodded.

"How long have you been studying Greek?" McGivens asked.

I hesitated again. But had to admit, "Never."

McGivens looked at the other two women. Some unspoken decision. Then she thanked me for my time and apologized again for her colleague and said someone would be in touch.

I was sure I'd blown it. Obviously. Do you ever see any of the interpreters at the UN suddenly screaming at some foreign dignitary during a session? No one would ever think I was cut out for the job.

But I guess … people are always on the lookout.

TED WHITLING: I am. I wish I'd found you first.

KIRSTEN SIMMENS: Well, that's nice.

TED WHITLING: I could have put you to work right away. But, anyway. Please go on. What happened next?

KIRSTEN SIMMENS: Military Intelligence. I got swept up. They were very, very flattering. I felt … good. Like I could make a real difference. It was a chance to serve my country. I really wanted to.

They started me out on small jobs. To be honest, I didn't tell them about my gift. I didn't explain it to anyone, the way I am to you now. And it's not like anyone really tried to explore it.

It was enough that they thought I could read minds. That's what they thought they were getting. I don't think anyone really understood what happened in that interview. That I could understand and yell at that General in a language I'd never learned.

As far as Military Intelligence knew, I was a mind-reader, and that was fantastic. A mind-reader who could speak a lot of languages. Even better.

So they put me to work in some low-level interrogations. I was supposed to just be inside the room while they did whatever they were doing, and then afterward I would tell them whatever the person they were interrogating was thinking.

TED WHITLING: How did that work out?

KIRSTEN SIMMENS: Not great. I was more of a distraction than they thought I would be. Not … physically. I'm not saying everyone was leering at me like the General and thinking only about me. It's not like I'm some bombshell.

I mean I was a mental distraction.

TED WHITLING: How so?

KIRSTEN SIMMENS: They knew I was in there, the people in custody. They knew I was in their minds, or … inside their language streams. It never happened with anyone who spoke English, but if anyone was thinking in some other language, I couldn't help but hear and respond. I couldn't figure out how to be invisible. It was a real nightmare. I couldn't make myself be silent.

So some of them would curse at me, which I could take pretty well, but if someone was begging me in his thoughts … it was just too hard. It was actually impossible. I didn't realize how sensitive I am. I couldn't bear people's pain— even when I knew they'd done horrible things. Things against our country, and that had gotten some of our men and women killed. I just wasn't tough enough, you know? I … flamed out. I was a wreck. Just a few months into the job and I had to quit.

TED WHITLING: And you were … twenty-six by then?

KIRSTEN SIMMENS: Twenty-seven. Washed out. No idea what to do next.

TED WHITLING: And then the offer at Base X. Can you tell me about that?

KIRSTEN SIMMENS: It was … extraordinary. I mean, almost unbelievable. I was pretty shocked at first.

I got the call after about a month of staying home and just trying to put myself back together. My mind felt like Swiss cheese. I didn't realize how much damage the whole experience was doing while it was going on. But afterward, my mind just felt raw and ragged. I stopped going out anywhere. I didn't want to accidentally step into anyone's language field. My parents brought me all my groceries. Even though I didn't move back home, they still took care of me.

Then Claire McGivens called me out of the blue. I still liked her. I appreciated how protective she was of me at that interview. I was no one. She could have sided with General Kosta and just thrown me out. But to throw him out instead. So I was happy to hear from her.

She said she knew a little about what happened with Military Intelligence, but maybe she had a better situation for me now.

I don't know what her connection was to all of it. I thought she just worked at the UN. But apparently that's just her day job. Or maybe cover of some kind. Because she recommended me for a top-top-secret interpreter job. As you know.

TED WHITLING: How did you react when you first met the extraterrestrials?

KIRSTEN SIMMENS: It's … hard to describe. I think it must be how mothers feel when they give birth and first look down at their babies. There's this intense—really intense—feeling of *This is mine. I'm going to protect it. I'm going to give up my whole life if I have to.*

I just wanted to hold them. To keep them safe. You've probably seen pictures of them, right? So you know how small they are, but it's their eyes. There's just something so compassionate and vulnerable there. And of course I could hear them talking, and I knew they were kind and gentle, and they were worried about what would happen to them. They asked for my help. Of course I would help them. The minute I met them, I was completely hooked. I'm glad I got the job, because it would have killed me to just leave them and walk away.

TED WHITLING: You weren't afraid.

KIRSTEN SIMMENS: No! How can you be afraid? They just wanted … connection, and love, and they wanted to understand. They were here to meet us. To reach out to us. I knew all of it just from our first ten minutes together. But then we talked all day and into the night. It was so intense, but just incredibly beautiful.

They told me their names, but I knew no one on the base would ever be able to pronounce them. So I gave them nicknames, just abbreviations. RJ, LX, and MT. The best I could do in translating their sounds into ours.

But once Reggie met them—

TED WHITLING: Reggie Swan. Sorry, just for the record.

KIRSTEN SIMMENS: Right. Reginald Swan. Base X tried out a few other Tech Specialists before they got to him, but once Reggie came, it was like an instant family. He renamed the guys, as he called them, RayJay, Linus, and Mit.

They loved him. I was a little jealous sometimes. They liked me fine, and I know they trusted me, but Reggie was just special to them. Like their long-lost brother. Different species, different galaxy, but somehow the four of them just belonged. I was on the outside, but I still got to be part of the whole experience. I … I just can't believe sometimes how lucky I was. It just changed my life.

TED WHITLING: Thank you for telling me all this, Ms. Simmens. I'm turning off the recording now. Interview over.

Ted clicked off the button on his recording device.

The two of us sat just looking at each other for a time.

"Are you reading my mind?" he asked.

I laughed. "No. But think in another language and I might."

He reached across the table and held my hand. I wasn't expecting it. We weren't close.

Then he let go, as if he just realized the same thing. He didn't apologize, he didn't seem embarrassed, but the moment passed.

But in that brief moment, while he held my hand and looked in my eyes, I know he was reading me. Not reading my mind, not inside a language field or anything I'm familiar with, but it was something palpable. As if he took something from me for a minute, then gave it back. It didn't feel creepy or intrusive. But it was noticeable.

"There are others," Ted said. "Like RayJay, Linus, and Mit."

My heart picked up speed. "Okay."

Already I felt the wash of some motherly instinct, returned. *Bring me more babies. I will love them too.*

I felt such a yearning. Because when the guys left, I wasn't prepared for that at all. One minute they were still there inside my mind, inside my field, and inside my heart

—and then suddenly I knew they were gone. Off the planet. Whoosh.

I felt such a ripping from my soul. I was afraid to let anyone know how bad it was. But it was a death and it was so sudden and I could barely stand it.

Even when Reggie Swan told me they were still alive but they had to go back to their own world. I couldn't believe they left without telling me goodbye.

As if our seven years together were nothing at all. Reggie was their friend, but apparently I wasn't.

Even though I thought of them all the time. I listened for them all the time. I wanted to talk to them every day the way we did that first day. Hours and hours, just listening to them tell me all about themselves and why they were here. Asking me to help them, so grateful when I said I would do everything in my power to make their life here as safe and happy as possible.

Ted Whitling waited for me to meet his gaze again. Then he nodded as if he understood it all.

"We would like you to start working for us out in the field," he said. "Not with aliens in custody, like at Base X. But hopefully keep them from ever being captured."

"But … the guys came here voluntarily," I told him. I didn't want to start off on the wrong foot, with a lie. RayJay and the other two were always clear that they sought out the base to bring their technology to share.

"My mistake," Ted said. "But the offer still stands. We would like you to help us communicate with any ETs trying to make contact. We would like to prevent some of the tragedies we've seen over the years."

I had heard rumors. Of extraterrestrials who weren't as lucky as the guys. Their crafts had been shot down, the ETs were captured or killed, their bodies dissected—it was too awful for words.

Some of the soldiers at Base X loved to tell me those stories just to see my face. Like you'd brag to someone that you strangled a puppy.

"Yes," I said quickly, as if the offer might expire in the next thirty seconds. "Yes," I told Ted Whitling, "I'd love to help you."

"It can be dangerous work, Kirsten. I want you to think about this. It isn't the kind of work you've been doing the past seven years."

The day that RayJay, Linus, and Mit escaped, Reggie and I weren't sure what was going to happen to us.

The Army wasn't happy to lose its prize specimens. Even though the guys left their valuable spacecraft behind.

Then Ted Whitling had shown up. I'd never heard of him before. He told Reggie and me that our time there had come to a close.

I honestly didn't know whether he was threatening us. I'd heard rumors of what happened to people who were no longer useful to Base X. I wondered if the two of us had suddenly become disposable.

But now, not only to find out no one wanted to get rid of me, but that they wanted me to do even more work with extraterrestrials—

"We'll need to train you," Ted said.

I smiled. "That's fine."

I thought of the little tow-headed three-year-old girl

with the purple crayon, coloring an elephant at her family's kitchen table.

Of the sadness I'd felt for my spaceman friend who was lost above our planet and trying to find his way home.

I thought of how responsible I must have felt. How much I wished I could help him if I could. But I was still too young and I didn't know how.

If there were others out there, speaking in consonants and vowels and clicks, or speaking in the smooth strange vibration of RayJay's and the other guys' language, then why else did I have this strange and specific gift? Why else was I here on Earth? Not to overhear lascivious generals thinking about my body in Greek.

I reached across the table in the small, close interview room, the same way Ted Whitling had reached across it to me. I could see he was sweating, even though I hadn't noticed it before. If he was nervous, I didn't want him to be.

I laid my hand on top of his and looked into his eyes. I could feel something leaving me for a moment, then coming back.

"What are you?" I whispered, narrowing my gaze. Because it was clear he wasn't just ordinary vanilla.

Ted smiled—maybe even a little sadly—and took back his hand. He pressed it against the table as he stood up.

"Ready to get started?" he asked.

I was. I needed something to fill the hole in my heart as quickly as possible.

I needed to look into other eyes like RayJay's and

Linus's and Mit's. I needed to feel the intense love I felt for them that first day.

What are you? I asked Ted. But someone could equally ask me that.

What am I? Just an interpreter. A linguist. A telepath who stands in the vibrating field of words and lets a language seep in through my skin and my heart and my mind. Any language, Earthbound or elsewhere. Friend to aliens and lost spacemen who beg for the help of a child to direct them back home.

Or beg for help once they're here. To tell them whether it's safe to stay or whether to flee. I've done that more than a few times now.

Ted Whitling was right. This work is dangerous. It's not like anything I've done before.

But I was born for it. Maybe even engineered for it, by the forces of nature and the needs of the future.

To look into the eyes of a being from elsewhere and know a love greater than any I've ever felt for a human, other than my parents.

Friend, mother, whatever this kind of love is, I want to feel it until the day I die.

Even if helping them is what might kill me.

There's a joke among the field agents. *I wouldn't mind dying on a mission—just not* this *mission.*

I understand that. But the where and when aren't mine to choose.

Until then, for as long as this lasts, I get stand in the waves of words and let them break over me. I get to swim in the ocean of knowledge. Dip my cup into it. Taste it.

Feel the wind and the water on my skin. I get to love and be loved by travelers from other places, from far away, searching for humans who will help them. One of those humans is me.

There are words for that, in every single language I've ever heard and understood and spoken.

Afortunada. Norocos. Glücklich. Onnekas.

Lucky.

INVITING

1

I meant to be far out of town long before anyone even knew to look for me.

Plans. Good luck to you. The best I can do anymore is have ideas, not plans. The world has changed too much. Just in the past four days.

I came by invitation to these remote mountains of Colorado, along with fifteen other scientists from around the country. The name of the conference sounded intriguing: *The Decade Ahead: Science at the Furthest Frontier*. The organizer, Dr. Adam Proul, a theoretical physicist like me, had a reputation for bringing together elite scientists from universities and the private sector to share in grand, visionary thinking.

Someone once said that the only way there is ever progress in science is when the older scientists with their entrenched theories finally start dying off.

I am old, by some measures, at the upper end of my

middle age, gray-haired and doughy, like a storybook grandmother. I could have retired already, but I have no desire. My mind is still as hungry as ever for knowledge.

I have always tried to push myself to see the new and to remain open to possibilities that might have sounded like fantasy even a year before.

So it did not surprise me to receive Dr. Proul's invitation. It seemed like a reward for my conscientious open-mindedness over all the long years of my teaching and publishing career, first at the University of Washington, and for the past fifteen years at the University of Wisconsin in Madison.

Dr. Proul's invitation described five days of deep learning and conversation among my colleagues over the Presidents' Day weekend at the end of February. *Bring warm clothing*, it said in the details. *A portion of the conference will take place outside.*

If I had known what that meant. Would I still have come here? If I knew everything that would happen.

Looking back is always dangerous. We must accept what we cannot change.

But no, I can't swear I would have done it. I would have been too terrified to try.

On our last night together as a group, after everything went to hell, Dr. Proul told us all we have one of two choices now: go into hiding, maybe for the rest of our lives. Or go public in a big, big way, hoping there's safety in being visible. There is no middle ground anymore, he said.

If he's right, then I'm going to try it both ways. Tell

what I know. Tell what I saw. Use it as insurance against disappearing at someone else's hands.

But then disappear on my own terms. Hide, just like Dr. Proul said.

Or at least try it. Ideas, not plans. I hope to God it will work.

2

It was afternoon by the time everyone arrived the first day. The place wasn't easy to get to. Some flew into Denver, some into the smaller airports at Gunnison or Montrose. All of us had to drive for a long time on steep, snowy roads.

The location was remote by design. Although at the time, I didn't understand that. It was in a luxury cabin owned by some billionaire donor, we were told. Someone who valued visionary ideas.

The house was spectacular, a huge three-story log cabin all by itself in the middle of fifty-five acres of rugged mountains and forest. There were twenty bedrooms and plenty of bathrooms—complete with steam showers and bidets—a workout room, an office suite with computers and a copier we were welcome to use, several meeting spaces, and a large open area on the first floor where the daily lectures would take place. We sat in comfortable chairs, like a high-end coffee shop, with stunning views of the snow-covered mountains out the surrounding windows.

Before the first lecture began we all introduced ourselves. I didn't know any of the other attendees. Several were from California—Caltech, Pepperdine, Stanford—and others were from universities on the east coast like Purdue and Cornell.

There was a woman who was a senior scientist at a telecommunications company in Lincoln, Nebraska, and a man who worked as a design engineer for an aircraft manufacturing company in Seattle.

Some of us were physicists, some chemists, engineers, an evolutionary biologist—we were an eclectic group.

I was by no means the oldest, but most of the scientists seemed to be in their forties and fifties. We were evenly split between men and women.

We were given delicious sandwiches for lunch, and dark, aromatic coffee. Then it was time for our first class. I chose one of the plush blue chairs near the back of the room, next to the fortyish woman from Pepperdine. I placed my spiral notebook and pen on my lap, and settled in to learn.

LEVEL I: PROJECTING

I liked the philosophy. I liked everything I heard. Dr. Proul spoke of things I realized I've been longing for all my life.

I am both a physicist and a metaphysicist at heart. My

father was a very religious man. He believed in the laying-on of hands.

He was a life insurance agent, the only one in our small town of Macon, Missouri. He and my mother brought up my younger sister Beth and me to believe in the power of prayer.

When I was thirteen, I watched the pastor of our small church cure my father of the tumor that was ravaging his lungs.

Maybe someone else would have gone into medicine after that. My sister became a massage therapist to learn to heal with her hands.

But I was always interested in knowing how the whole universe worked. Not just the human body, or the mind, or the soul.

And so when Dr. Adam Proul stood before us that first day, with his tall, athletic bearing and his feathery brown hair laced with strands of gray, and he smiled in an almost bashful way as he described his three-level protocol, I found myself surprisingly ready to do what he asked.

We were to sit quietly for the next hour, comfortable in our wide, cushioned chairs, feet tucked up under us, if that felt best, but however we wanted to do it. We were to close our eyes and give ourselves over to a new vision. A vision of each of our own making.

"Choose the future you want to project yourself into," said Dr. Proul. "Ten years from today. We begin that future this minute. Ignore all the reasons why it can't be the way you want. Right now, none of those obstacles exist.

"Think of every single aspect of the world you want us to have," he said. "New advancements in medicine. Technology. Transportation. Environment. Space exploration. Inventions. The political situation. If you want people to live in peace with each other, imagine that. If you want all Earthlings to be united, imagine that. If you want us to already be traveling among the planets, picture that."

I looked around the room to see how some of the other scientists were reacting. Some chuckled, as if they were a little embarrassed by what he was saying. But most of them looked as intrigued as I was.

It wasn't like a guided meditation. I've done those here and there over the years.

This was an appeal to our scientific, theoretical minds. Dr. Proul was serious. He wanted us to invent a new world.

He wanted the man who designed planes to stop worrying whether he would ever get the funding to do all that he imagined. He wanted the evolutionary biologist to project our species into a better future.

He wanted me, Dr. Angela Corliss, to explore all my ideas about zero-point energy and quantum fields, and my pet project, Pure Dark Energy, and leap over all the impedimenta that were currently holding me back.

My concerns about use by the military. My fights with the physics department about funding for my research lab. All the day-to-day hassles of the real world that were impinging on my blissful theoretical world of free, clean, infinite energy just waiting all around us to be harvested.

To imagine that I had already accomplished a decade

from now what I've been imagining for the past forty years.

That hour of projecting was delightful.

When Dr. Proul quietly told us our hour was over, I only reluctantly returned to the world. The room was still warm, with a duskier light now that the sun was already behind the high mountains.

The people around me rose slowly, groggily, some of them stretched and groaned about their stiff joints, but everyone seemed equally content. As though we had all just bathed in soothing clear pools and now were ready to face our real lives again.

But this wasn't my real life. For the first time in a long time, I felt pampered. Everything was taken care of. Everything was easy.

An early dinner awaited us in the second floor dining area, prepared by a smiling staff of chefs. The food was both delicious and artistic. Gorgeous salads and appetizers. I had a slice of quiche that belonged in a Renaissance painting. There were glasses of wine for whoever wanted them, but I was happy with another cup of dark coffee. There was one more class after dinner, and I wanted to stay alert.

Dr. Proul suggested we rest in our rooms for half an hour before coming back downstairs for more.

I climbed up the wide log staircase to my bedroom on the third floor. The room was quaint and woodsy, everything done in knotty pine. There was a warm patch quilt on the bed. I pulled it over my legs and sat in bed making notes about everything that had come to me while I projected myself into the future.

A future where my free, pure energy was already powering everything that currently depended on gas and oil and coal. I had made lists like that before, but this one felt different. I wasn't just hoping things would change, I was pretending I had actually accomplished it.

I felt relieved that I didn't have to fight for it anymore. It was here. Everyone agreed and wanted what I had to give them.

After what felt like only a few minutes, I heard a soft chime floating up from downstairs. It was time for the second class. I was hungry for what Dr. Proul would have us explore next.

LEVEL TWO: ASSUMING

"Why was Benjamin Franklin alive at the time of the Revolutionary War?" Dr. Proul asked us. "Why was Lincoln alive during a time of slavery? We are born in these times on purpose," Dr. Proul said. "Just as those who were born during the time of the Civil War or the discovery of penicillin or the days of Thoreau and Emerson were born in those times on purpose."

"Why?" one of the men asked. The professor from Cornell, I think.

Dr. Proul smiled. "So that all of us can add to the forward momentum of our times by seeing clearly where we can go."

He gave us the example of being alive when the Wright Brothers first flew at Kitty Hawk in 1903. "Why did they believe they could build and fly an airplane?" Dr. Proul asked. "Because it was *time.* Enough people believed it was possible by then. You don't know their names, you have no idea who they were, where they lived, what their professions were, where they worshipped, what they believed about anything else, but we know that the belief had been building for a long time. Look at Leonardo da Vinci's flying machine designs back in the 1400s. It took much longer to bring to life than he must have ever imagined, but eventually the time was here. And it was because by then enough people *believed.*"

I wasn't sure that he was right, but I liked the story nonetheless. I could imagine all those faceless men and women in a crowd, all of them sparking the same idea that humans could fly somehow, that such a machine could actually exist. I understood Dr. Proul's theory.

"And so now I ask the same of you," he said. He was standing before us again, at the front of the open room. The shades were all drawn to keep out the darkness, and the lighting felt mellow and warm and cocooning.

But I wasn't sleepy. I was wide awake, hanging on his words. If I were reading a book with all of this, I would have stayed up past my bedtime to keep going.

My fellow scientists were all awake and listening, too, even the ones I noticed having several glasses of wine. I preferred another mug of that same dark coffee I'd enjoyed in the afternoon, this time with a splash of hot chocolate and the offered tower of whipped cream.

I cupped the mug in my hands as I listened. I left my spiral notebook and pen on the floor. This was a time to absorb, not record. I was trying to guess where he was going with all this.

Dr. Proul pushed up the sleeves of his tan wool sweater as if this topic were overheating him, firing him from within. I was leaning forward in my chair, listening hard. I was ready to try the next experiment.

"Believe that you are alive in these times for a reason," he said. "Believe that you are modern scientists at exactly the right time.

"And now for the next hour I ask you to assume that this is true. Not only imagine it. I want us all to discuss the great many advantages to being alive specifically now. Why is your work finally ready to be used by the human race? Why now and not five years ago or ten or twenty?"

Dr. Proul pointed at the woman from the telecommunications company in Nebraska. She was in her mid-forties, with ash blonde hair cut in a stylish blunt bob that brushed along the line of her jaw. She was one of the few women in the room wearing make up. She had arrived wearing an elegant dark tailored suit with a light blue knit sweater underneath it, and a thin gold necklace and matching earrings.

Whereas I wore what I usually do in the Wisconsin winters, dressing for warmth rather than style. Fleece-lined relaxed jeans and a waffle long john top beneath my red flannel overshirt. I long ago gave up trying to be cute or impress anyone. But the woman from Nebraska looked attractive and clearly corporate.

"Sheila?" Dr. Proul addressed her. "Why is this the exactly right time for you?"

I could see Sheila's blush from across the room. She wasn't expecting to be called on like a student.

But she rallied. And in a voice that shook a little with nerves, she told us, "I-I had a particular design. I've been working on it for over ten years. But I could never solve one particular issue with the functionality. Until … well, until last year. The part that I needed was suddenly invented by someone in Italy. Ever since then…" She smiled now as she gazed around the group. "It works. Simply and beautifully. So yes," she told Dr. Proul, "I think I understand what you mean."

"Bob?" he said, turning to the chemist from the University of Chicago. "Why are you here in these times? Why is this the right time for your work?"

Bob regaled us with a technical answer that once again seemed to hinge on someone else's discovery just a few years ago.

Then it was my turn to be called on. "Angela?"

I had had time to think of my answer.

"I think I am here in these specific times because of all the television shows. Especially *Star Trek* and *Star Wars*."

That brought a laugh from the others, although I didn't intend it that way. I was serious. I could see it very clearly.

"It's what you said," I told Dr. Proul. "Asking ourselves why our work is finally ready to be used by the human race. First they had to be prepared by television and movies so they would accept it."

Sheila from Nebraska caught my eye and gave me a

smile. I saw a few other scientists nodding in agreement. But some rolled their eyes, like I'd said something so juvenile. I knew I was right. I continued with my theory.

"If I tried to convince someone they could power their cars and homes with free, clean, pure energy—energy that's all around us right now—if I'd tried to tell people that in the 1930s or 1950s, no one would have understood what I was talking about. But think of all the inventions we accept because we've seen them on science fiction shows. Space travel, smart phones, computers of all kinds. The human race had to prepare their brains first."

Dr. Proul pointed at me and said, "Exactly." I felt like he'd given me a gold star.

This was a conversation I'd never had with any of my physics colleagues before, even though I had thought about it privately often enough.

Every time I saw some invention in a futuristic universe, I knew in my heart that if some writer or designer could make that up, it meant that a scientist like me could actually create it. For some reason, ever since my childhood, I've always taken that on absolute faith. That if someone could think an idea, that idea was now out there in the world and alive, just waiting for someone smart and brave enough to give it a tangible existence.

Maybe it came from watching my father healed by the laying-on of hands. Our pastor had the idea that he could do it and he did. My father lived to be ninety-five after that, even though lung cancer wanted to kill him at the age of forty-one.

Why did that pastor believe? Where did he get the idea?

It must have been because he had seen or heard of someone else doing it, too. Or maybe he even saw in some old-time movie, I don't know.

A movie was what set me on my own path.

During my third year of undergrad at Princeton, I took myself to a movie all alone on a Saturday night. It wasn't particularly good, but that didn't matter. There was a scientist who had discovered what he called Pure Dark Energy. He had a long corny speech about what it was. Maybe no one in the theater gave it even a half a second's thought.

But as a physics student I was electrified.

I was there that night to catch that specific spark. I know it. I have no doubt. I didn't read about it in a textbook. I didn't hear about it from my professors. I went out looking for it because of some science fiction writer's idea.

And now decades later I have found that Pure Dark Energy truly exists. And I am ready to teach the world how to use it.

Despite, as Dr. Proul said, the various obstacles in my way: lack of funding, lack of support—even the outright scorn from my peers.

"We are here in these times," Dr. Proul said, "because we can see advancements that our fellow humans haven't imagined yet. And we are here to move the human race forward as far as we can during our own lifetimes. We might not be the Wright Brothers who actually accomplish what we feel so passionately we're here to do. But we might be the people who lived right before those two boys were born, and who already believed that what they intended to do in the future was absolutely possible."

Dr. Proul looked around the room. "Does that energize you or disappoint you?"

"You mean the idea that I'm the guy who came before the Wright Brothers, but I'm not them?" said the evolutionary biologist named Jorge. "Yes, that depresses me. I want to live to see my work matter."

"All right," said Dr. Proul, "then tell us why you are alive in these times. Why now?"

Jorge sighed. His face was lined with a combination of age and maybe worry. He might have been around my age or slightly older. He had thick brown hair with a noticeable strip of gray on the right side, as if someone had painted it there and left the rest of his head untouched.

"I am alive in these times..." Jorge repeated. Then he sighed again. As if delaying the moment when he would tell us the truth.

Dr. Proul watched him closely with a new kind of intensity I hadn't seen in him before. He had invited Jorge to the conference. There must be a reason. Dr. Proul must have known what the scientist would say.

"I have seen things," Jorge said. "Since I was a little boy growing up in Columbia. I have seen..." He smiled wryly. "Our neighbors."

Dr. Proul leaned back against the table at the front of the room. Maybe signaling that he was yielding the floor and was ready to hear the story.

"Why am I alive in these times?" Jorge said. "Because if I was born any earlier or later, I would have missed it. There have been spaceships coming to Earth for centuries, maybe millennia. But cameras … they have been recording them for only so long. Making a record and giving us proof."

"Spaceships," muttered the engineer from Purdue.

"Yes," Jorge said with a defiant bite to his voice. "Our gray friends. I met my first one when I was just a boy. I have met more than forty others since then."

The room fell silent. There was a thickness to the air. There was no clock on the wall, but I swear I could hear one ticking.

"You talk about assuming," Jorge said to Dr. Proul. "Assuming that what we believe is true. When you see something with your own eyes, you don't have to assume, you know."

"Exactly," said Dr. Proul. Another gold star. "When you know, you know, and that's it." He stopped leaning back on the table and stood up straight again. There was a certain confidence in his posture.

"I know, too," he told us. "I have spoken with *our gray friends*, as Jorge calls them. I have spoken with many others, too. They are all around us."

"And here we go…" said Bob the chemist. He folded his arms over his oversized belly and shook his head in pompous disbelief.

As if he just realized he had been tricked into coming all this way for some kind of fringe event.

But Dr. Proul was not deterred. He smiled at the chemist and held out his right hand as though inviting Bob to shake it. But instead it became a different gesture.

An inviting kind of gesture. As in, *Okay, then, let's go see.*

"You all have your coats? Ready to bundle up?" asked Dr. Proul.

We guests looked around at one another. We weren't sure what was happening.

Dr. Proul consulted his watch. "This would be a good time. Please, everyone, go grab your coats. Get changed into something warmer if you need to. I'd like to meet back here in about fifteen minutes."

He didn't linger, maybe guessing that we wouldn't move if he did. He strode out of the room and left us to ourselves.

I didn't hesitate. I was excited to see what came next. So I picked up my spiral notebook and pen and empty mug and headed back up the log staircase to my room on the third floor.

My heart was beating fast. Happiness, anticipation— something new. Not just my everyday life anymore. New ideas and new energy. I was so glad I came all this way, even though I hadn't been sure it would be worth all the effort.

Some workshops and conferences promise big ideas and big change. But in my experience, they rarely deliver it. I've left professional work events feeling deflated more times than I can remember.

But this. It just felt different. I couldn't change into my warmer clothes fast enough.

I pulled on a pair of long johns to wear under my jeans and added a thick fleece sweater over my flannel shirt. Then I zipped into my bright teal ski coat. I'd been wearing it for the past several winters, since it seemed to keep out the brutal wind better even than my long puffy down coat.

When I returned to the lecture space on the first floor, only a few of the other scientists were there.

One of them was Sheila from Nebraska. She, too, knew how to dress for a serious winter. She had changed out of her tailored, elegant suit, and now wore insulated black ski pants, a thick ivory-colored cable knit sweater, and a heavy blue ski jacket over that. As I walked into the room she was just pulling on a lavender knit hat that came down low over her ears.

"What do you think?" I asked her quietly. I remembered her catching my eye and nodding after I shared my theory that movies and television prepared our fellow humans to accept radical new advances in science.

"I think ... we'll see," she said with a kind of thrill in her voice.

Then more of our colleagues came to join us.

I noticed that a few of them were still missing. But as the minutes went by, I wondered if that was deliberate.

Dr. Proul returned, too, wearing serious outdoor gear. Heavy boots, a heavy coat, a thick fleece hat.

He gazed around the room, then took the absences in stride: Bob the chemist, the man who worked for the aircraft manufacturer in Seattle, and the woman from Pepperdine.

Dr. Proul led our group of thirteen outside onto the wrap-around porch. There were Adirondack chairs out there for sitting and staring out at the magnificent view.

But we didn't stop there. We weren't going to be sitting.

Dr. Proul continued leading us down the three steps from the porch onto the snowy bib in front of the house. Then he turned right and continued walking along a path that someone else had already made through the snow after the blustery storm I had watched out the windows that afternoon.

There were no lights outside. Dr. Proul didn't even carry a flashlight. But the half-clouded moon and the snow all around us brightened the darkness enough that we could see where we were going.

There were sprinkles of stars up above, very beautiful on a frigid cold night. The temperature must have been somewhere between zero and ten. I could tell by the way the hairs in my nostrils froze after just a few breaths. I have lived through my share of cold dark winters.

No one spoke for a while. We concentrated on our footing. Our boots squeaked on the freshly fallen snow.

I could see my breath fogging in front of my face. I loved the feeling of the crisp cold air. I loved the stark white of the snow-capped mountains against the dark of the sky.

But I was glad for my insulated mittens. Sheila from Nebraska wore a pair of thin leather gloves that she clapped together every few minutes to try to warm her hands.

Some of the other scientists seemed underdressed, too. Particularly the ones from California.

After a while I could hear a low murmur from up ahead. Dr. Proul and Jorge the evolutionary biologist spoke together in quiet tones.

I felt a little left out. I would have loved to hear what the two were saying. Sheila must have felt that way, too, because she dropped back to walk beside me so she could whisper, "Do you believe him? About seeing spaceships and little gray men?"

"A hundred percent," I said. "You?"

Sheila chuckled softly. She patted her gloved hands together again and then briefly held them over her cold cheeks and mouth.

"I think," she said, "I'd like to see one myself."

"So you believe it's possible."

Sheila said, "Oh, yes."

We both hurried to keep up. I think we both wanted to move closer to Jorge and Dr. Proul to hear what they were saying. But there wasn't time before Dr. Proul stopped and turned to face the group.

By then we were standing on a levelled patch of snow. It looked like it might have been cleared with a snow blower. The area was round and about as big as the first floor room that we'd just left. Big enough that sixteen scientists and the conference leader could comfortably stand in a group. Since we were fewer, there was plenty of room.

"Ten years ago," said Dr. Proul, "I stood exactly where we're standing now. There was no house yet, only this land.

"I'll tell you the truth. I felt lost that night. I was living in a world I didn't want to believe had fallen so far from my expectations. Political turmoil, a new war on the horizon, a feeling of just plain meanness among my fellow humans. Maybe some of you have felt that same way."

There was a soft murmur of assent from the group, including me. I have definitely being feeling that lately.

This sense that for as long as I've been alive I've seen such incredible advancements in technology and science, and yet humanity itself could still be so primitive and barbaric.

"So I sat right here on a cold dark night," said Dr. Proul, "and I talked to the stars and I talked to myself. And I asked myself, if I could project myself into a better future, what would it look like? How would it be different—not only different, but better?

"And then I put myself into that future. I assumed everything I saw was real. I assumed that it already existed, and I just had to find my way into it. A future me had already forged the path, and now he was reaching back to me and asking me to follow in his footsteps and come meet him."

He paused then, to let his words take hold. They certainly took hold of me. The idea that there was a future me already doing what I've dreamed of. And that she was reaching back to me—I could imagine her smiling at me, encouraging me—and saying, *Come on, now. I've already done it. Just come this way. Meet me.*

But even though an idea like that might seem radical and fanciful, as a theoretical physicist I was used to stretching my mind. Engaging in thought experiments, as Albert Einstein used to call them. It was how he came up with his theory of relativity.

But I understood that what Dr. Proul was suggesting might feel too *out there* for some of the others. I was glad Bob the chemist wasn't with us. Maybe he would have scoffed. Called it fantasy. Said he was going back to the house for more wine.

Instead, everyone in our assembled group silently absorbed Dr. Proul's story. I could feel a united kind of energy among us.

"And then," said Dr. Proul more quietly than before, "something shifted inside me. And right at that moment, I knew what I could do."

LEVEL III: INVITING

The temperature felt like it had dropped even a few more degrees. The clouds had blown past, and the sky was dark and clear. I could see a plane with its blinking red light flying high above the snow-covered peaks in the distance. But down here on Earth where the other scientists and I stood gathered together on the cleared patch of snow, everything felt quiet and still and peaceful. There was a feeling of reverence. Like the way church felt when I was young when I first stepped inside the doors on Sunday mornings.

For just a moment, maybe only five seconds at most, all time and activity would feel suspended. As if I had stepped into a pocket of space and time where there was nothing but the great Void, just the soft quiet womb of darkness beyond the commotion of our regular world.

Then, inevitably, the world would rush back in. I would

hear the organ playing and hear the murmurs of the congregation as people chatted before the service began. The peace and the silence were broken.

But I never forgot those few seconds of suspended time. That was my first real experience of magic. Of the mystical. I suppose I've been searching for it ever since.

And now here it was again, that same feeling as though time had stopped for a moment or two while the other scientists and I stood on the cleared circle of snow and watched our breath fog on the air and let Dr. Proul's story about the future weave its magic, preparing us for what might happen next.

It was Dr. Proul himself who broke into the silence. He turned to the evolutionary biologist. "Jorge," he said quietly, "you told us you want to live to see your work matter."

"Yes," Jorge said. "That's right."

"Tell us," said Dr. Proul. "What is your work?"

"Basically," Jorge said, "it is studying the history of life forms here on Earth."

"No," Dr. Proul pressed him, "what is your *specific* work?"

Jorge drew in a cold breath. I could see it fog out again in front of him. He spread his gloved hands, as if appealing to all of us. For what? Understanding? Mercy? Kindness?

I looked at Sheila. She widened her eyes in response. We both wanted desperately to hear what Jorge would say.

"Because of what I saw when I was a boy," he said. "I know that others have been on Earth for a long time. Longer than I have been alive, I'm certain of it. I have found … artifacts. And remains. And other proof. They lived here before, and they live here now. In hidden places I have been able to uncover. But people are afraid to know it."

"Aliens," one of the other scientists said. I think it was Claudette, the physicist from Caltech. She sounded like she hoped she was guessing wrong.

"Friends," Jorge corrected her. "Not what they show in scary movies. They aren't here to attack us or abduct us or mutilate our cows." Then he looked at me. "But it's what you said, Dr. Corliss. About movies and TV. They shape our minds. They tell us what to expect. And I think the people in power have been lying to us for years."

"I agree," said Dr. Proul. "They want us to be afraid. They don't want us to try to make contact."

"Why?" Sheila asked.

"It's because of *War of the Worlds*," someone said. "People panicked over that radio show. They thought aliens had really invaded. After that, the government decided it was too dangerous to tell us the truth."

I had heard that same explanation before, too. How Orson Welles did an adaptation of the H.G. Wells story some time in the 1930s, and listeners were convinced that Martians had really landed in New Jersey.

After watching their mass panic, the government decided to withhold any evidence of actual alien encounters. People would lose their minds if they knew it was real. So starting with the UFO crash in Roswell, New Mexico in the 1940s, they've been covering up alien visitation here ever since.

Or so I'd heard. I think it was common knowledge.

But Dr. Proul gave us a different explanation. "It's all about money. And power. And greed."

In the past ten years of inviting scientists to his conferences, he'd learned a lot about the secret workings of the government and military and the ultra-wealthy.

Yes, aliens had landed here. To try to make contact. To try to forge a relationship with the human race.

And their ships were attacked. The pilots were killed or captured. Live aliens were kept prisoner in underground facilities for years.

Their spacecrafts were torn apart and studied inch by inch. Their methods of engineering and design were copied and tested by the top minds all around the world.

Dr. Proul looked at me across the cold expanse where we stood. "Your ideas about Pure Dark Energy. Where did they come from?"

"A movie," I said. "Back when I was in college."

"That may have given you the idea," Dr. Proul said, "but you've been researching it for years. How do you know you're right?"

"Because … I've made things," I answered. "It works. It's real." I could have told them all about my decades of research and experimentation. But I didn't want to take up time. I wanted to hear what Dr. Proul and Jorge said instead. I already knew what I know. I wasn't there to teach. I was there to learn.

"How long ago did you know?" Dr. Proul asked.

"Twenty years," I said. "Maybe twenty-five."

"And yet we're still powering our world with oil and

gas," he said. "When you could have given us free, pure energy that long ago."

It was a source of great friction between my physics peers and me. But again, I didn't want to waste time going into it.

"Everyone here," said Dr. Proul, "has found a piece of the ultimate puzzle. This is why I asked you to come. Because the future I asked you to project yourself into is already here, already available, we just have to ask."

And with that, he turned his back to us and held up his arms to the sky.

And then Dr. Jorge Diaz stood beside him and did the same.

And for some reason, although I couldn't explain where I got the nerve, I walked up to stand beside them and lifted my arms, too.

All around the clearing, the other scientists joined us in the gesture. I doubt that any of them knew any more than I did what might happen.

But a light dropped from the sky, like a ball of glowing fire. It was the size of a basketball, colored bright reddish orange.

It hovered in the cold air above us, maybe fifty feet off the snow, and then it began to grow and expand and change colors.

It flattened from its sphere to take on a wider, triangular shape. Like looking at one of the experimental stealth planes I've seen in articles over the years. But those planes are dark gray, and this ship—for that's what it was—was rimmed all along the bottom in rapidly moving lights, red and green and white, that lit up the pale gray exterior and made it take on each of those colors in turn.

And still it continued to expand. Until it reached a size twice as large as the circle where we all stood.

It hovered above us. My neck was starting to hurt from tipping my head back for so long. But I rubbed the muscles and continued watching.

Then poor Claudette, the physicist from Caltech, started to scream. She was staring at the ship and absolutely freaking out. It was here, it was real, and she couldn't stand it.

I went to her and tried to calm her down. But she was hysterical. She was hyperventilating and still she screamed.

I didn't know what to do. But Dr. Proul must have seen a reaction like that before. He did something I never would have expected.

He took off his heavy coat and threw it over Claudette's head. Then he hugged her to him and began talking her down.

I saw someone do that with their dog at a Fourth of July party one year. The fireworks were sending the dog into a spiral. But the owner calmly threw a blanket over the dog, then held him and rocked him and spoke to him sweetly.

It worked for the dog, and much to my amazement it worked with Claudette. Soon the coat came off her head and she was able to breathe normally.

She looked deeply embarrassed. But I noticed she avoided looking up. The ship was still there. She must have known it, but she didn't have to see it.

But I wanted to see it. Absolutely. The lights were beautiful to watch. They circled around the rim of the craft, changing from red to green to white, all three, during every pass.

I kept expecting … something. Like a hatch opening. A long runway coming down. Something like an emergency chute on an airplane.

I had watched enough science fiction movies and TV, I knew how aliens exited their crafts.

Except I didn't. Without any change in the exterior of the ship, suddenly I saw a bright green light weaving among us.

A light that felt palpable. Of substance. *Cellular*, somehow. Not cellular like a phone, but like an organism comprised of bright green living cells.

Cells that stretched and moved and wove their way through the gathered humans, maybe smelling us, feeling us, I didn't know.

I took off my right glove and lifted my bare hand just in time to touch the light as it passed for a second time. Whatever it was was warm against my skin.

And it paused as we connected. It felt me and knew I was reaching out.

And I felt something leave me, through my skin, out of my hand.

Just a slight jolt of energy, no more. It wasn't as though the light drained me or sucked me dry.

It took only enough to let me know that our touch was real. I wasn't imagining it. It wasn't just a moving, formless light.

And a split-second later, after I felt the jolt of something leave, I felt the smooth entrance of something new. Coming through my fingertips, a kind of energy that was foreign to me. Not of my body. Not of anything I'd ever felt.

It smoothed through my fingers, across my palm, and then up my forearm to my shoulder. Like a loved one clasping me warmly and fondly gazing into my eyes.

I felt the creature's gaze, looking deeply into my own. But it wasn't the light, it was the smooth feeling of energy inside my hand and arm. The body parts didn't match the sensation I received. It would be like expressing your love to someone by rubbing static on the bottom of their feet.

Claudette must have been watching my expression, because she must have assumed that it was safe. She held up her right hand, too. And this time, rather than dissolving into hysterics and hyperventilation, she gasped once and then visibly relaxed.

Everyone took a turn after that. Holding up their palms, giving what the light took and receiving what it gave.

Dr. Proul took his turn last. He had obviously done it before. Maybe many, many times.

He closed his eyes and smiled at the interaction. He held up both of his hands and intermingled with the bright green light.

Jorge had shifted his position within the circle, and was standing close enough to me that I could whisper to him.

"Have you ever seen this before?"

"No," he said. "But it's beautiful, isn't it?" He turned to me and smiled and I could see tears glistening in his eyes.

After a time, and too soon as far as all of us were concerned, the light melted back into the darkness. A hatch never opened, a chute never slid out of a door, but I knew the visitor had returned to the ship.

We watched the ship contract again, growing smaller and changing shape. And the color returned to the glowing orange ball.

And in that configuration, small enough that one projectile could do it, a shot cracked through the air and a bullet fired at the ship.

We all turned at the sound. It was a shock to my heart. To go from such beauty and peace to sudden violence.

Bob the chemist stood in his heavy canvas coat holding a pistol of some kind and looking scared.

He fired it again. And a third time. And then finally people started to move. One of the men bowled into him and knocked him to the ground.

Two of the other men jumped on top of him. One of them wrested away his gun and threw it out into the snow.

There were curses then, lots of shocked and angry shouts.

And through it all, Dr. Proul stood in front of the glowing orange sphere.

He had moved there after the sound of the first shot. He held up his arms as if trying to shield it.

But I could see now a dark stain on the side of his neck.

He didn't seem to know it was there.

But his body knew it well. Dr. Proul collapsed into the snow. I ran to him. Blood was pouring out.

"Call someone!" Sheila shouted. "Go back to the house! Call!"

But people had cell phones. A few of them whipped them out.

"No service," one of the men said. Then he took off running back toward the house. Everything seemed to be moving at a dangerously slow pace.

Dr. Proul was unconscious. I wasn't surprised. One of the bullets had torn through the side of his neck.

I pulled off my glove and pressed my hand there, applying pressure. I could feel hot blood pulsing against my palm.

But I could feel something else. Because it was the hand that I'd used to invite the light in. And it had responded to my call.

The glowing orange sphere still hovered above where Dr. Proul now lay. And I knew that inside it the intelligence was experiencing this right along with me.

Other scientists gathered around in a circle, asking questions, making suggestions, some of them moaning in dismay.

But I didn't need any of them. I was someplace else.

Light moved from deep inside my heart and lungs. It moved out through my arm and then my hand.

It burrowed into the wound in Dr. Proul's neck. It spread the same way I had felt it spread through me, delivering the strange new energy.

I thought of the pastor in my childhood church. The way he closed his eyes and lifted his face to heaven.

How he recited his prayer and kept his hand steady on

my father's chest. How the pastor never faltered, never doubted that he could do what he intended to do.

I projected myself into a future when some alien energy could heal a human's flesh. I assumed I could do it. I had seen the pastor heal my father. I had felt the light change me as it entered my hand.

I invited it in, this alien presence hovering above. I accepted the gift that I knew it could offer.

Was it because I had seen some movie like this? Read it in some book? Or was it because I knew it by my own experience, just from feeling it moving out of me and into Dr. Proul?

I knew I could heal him, and I did. There on the cold, blood-stained snow. We didn't need a doctor. We didn't need outside help of any kind.

Bob the chemist, who had shot at the sphere and hit Dr. Proul instead, vomited when he saw our host sit up.

One of the men kicked him in the ribs as he was retching into the snow. I didn't mind, even though I felt peaceful and not inclined to do violence.

Dr. Proul reached out his hand toward the glowing sphere. He didn't touch it, it was a little too high above us.

He held his hand there for a moment, and then the sphere shot away.

I could hear the sound of scientists breathing, as if someone had suddenly turned up the volume on just that one noise.

"What do we do about Bob?" someone asked.

"It's already done," said Dr. Proul.

I didn't know what that meant, but from the look on Bob the chemist's face, it obviously scared him.

"Why did you shoot it?" Sheila asked.

"None of your business," Bob said.

But I assumed it was because he was afraid. He wasn't with us, he didn't feel what we felt. He saw something *other*, and like the primitive barbarian that he was, he could only try to hurt it, shoot it, kill it.

But I was wrong. Just shows how naïve I've been. Dr. Proul tried to tell us before all of it happened, but I must not have been listening.

3

It was a strange and somber scene after that. All of us were shaken. All of us were still trying to process everything we'd seen and felt.

Everyone in the group, except for Bob the chemist, had felt the touch of the green alien light. We knew that it was real.

And we knew that it was good. It meant us no harm. Just like Dr. Proul told us. It was only Bob the barbarian who brought violence and chaos.

The men who had tackled him and wrestled the gun out of his hands must have felt some duty to keep guarding him, because the two of them kept a firm grip on Bob's arms while they yanked him back along the path to the house.

I stayed behind. I wasn't ready to speak to anyone yet. I needed the clear cold darkness and the muffling snow and time, mostly time.

But I did not get my wish. I was not alone. There were four of us still standing in the clearing after all the others began walking in a slow, stiff stupor behind Bob and his escorts.

Dr. Proul, Jorge, Sheila, and I found ourselves standing in a private, informal circle.

We all looked at one another for a moment of suspended time.

Then Dr. Proul moved. He reached across the distance between us and took my hand in his. I had put my thick gloves back on by then, and the one on the right had already sopped up what was left of Dr. Proul's blood on my hand. The inside of the glove still felt moist.

"You saved my life." Dr. Proul whispered it. I was glad. I wasn't ready to hear a full-volume voice.

There was no point in acting modest, in denying it, in saying, *Aw, shucks, anyone coulda done it.* I nodded. It was true. I did save him. But we all knew I didn't do it on my own.

Dr. Proul glanced over his shoulder, up into the sky. Maybe confirming that the orange round sphere was still somewhere out of sight, safe.

"What did you feel?" Jorge Diaz asked me.

I removed my hand from its bloody glove and pressed it against my right cheek.

My fingers still felt warm. Warm because of the light they took in when the alien passed me. I held out my hand to each of the three of them in turn and let them feel my warmth against their cheeks.

I didn't say anything. What was there to say? I put my

hand back inside the wet glove. The cold of it made me shiver.

"So what now?" Jorge asked Dr. Proul. "What happens to that psychopath?"

"What did you mean?" I asked, finally testing the strength of my voice. It sounded far away to my own ears. "You said, *It's already done.* What does that mean?"

"Sometimes I make mistakes," said Dr. Proul. "About who I invite here. Obviously I made a mistake with him."

That didn't answer my question, but I didn't feel like pressing it. I was starting to feel cold. The alien warmth was fading fast.

Sheila had been standing with us all that time, but I hadn't heard her say a word.

I looked at her now. Her eyes seemed bright, like pinpoints of starlight reflected off the crystalline snow.

"Are you all right?" I asked her. Earlier, when I let each of them feel my warm fingers against their cheeks, I thought I felt Sheila tremble. But she didn't seem afraid, maybe just cold. My warm fingers set off a reaction on her chilled skin.

Sheila nodded. "We should go back."

"Yes," said Dr. Proul. "I need to speak to everyone."

"Can we … will you wait just a moment?" Jorge asked.

He tipped back his head and looked up at the stars. Then he folded his hands against his chest, pressing his palms into his heart. "Did you feel it? All of you? The way it spoke to you, into your heart?"

We all murmured *Yes* together. Until Jorge asked us, I don't think I remembered that that was what I felt.

But he was right. The green living light did speak to me, into my heart. Its touch was gentle and emotional and very loving.

I don't know that I would have described it that way to a single scientist that I knew, but since Jorge asked, I felt it was important to tell the truth.

When I shared that description, Jorge the evolutionary biologist nodded. "That is how I have felt every time. Do you see? They are good. They want connection. They don't want to harm us."

"And then Bob shot at it," I said. I felt nothing but disgust. Even if the man had been scared, there was no need to respond with a gun.

"It's who we are," Dr. Proul said. "At least some of us. You can see what we have to overcome. But it's why I invite people here. And why I invite them..." He gestured behind him into the sky where the ship had disappeared. "I could sit out here every night and simply commune with them by myself. But I have to bring humanity along. You can see that, can't you? Otherwise we don't ever reach the future I'm projecting myself into."

I suppose someone else listening to that explanation might have thought Dr. Proul was somewhat insane. At a minimum, delusional. He had taken his fantasy idea and made the mistake of believing it was real.

But the thing was, it was real. Everything that had just happened was absolutely concrete fact. A group of thirteen scientists and our leader Dr. Proul had stood in this clearing in the snow and held out our arms and invited an alien ship to come down and meet us.

An alien presence then mingled among us. That was real. We all felt it.

A man had shot Dr. Proul in the neck. He was bleeding out. That happened.

Then I. I did what I did. I was a conduit. I was a tool.

And the man who should be dead was now standing across from me, completely healed.

What part of that was a fantasy taken too far?

But where do you go from there, after you've experienced something miraculous?

How do you talk about it to anyone outside?

How do you just return to things as they were, and not change your worldview after what you've seen?

You don't, is the answer. And I should know it.

When I was thirteen years old, my father was so weak from his cancer, my mother and my younger sister and I had to help support him as he made his slow, painful way into our church.

It wasn't a Sunday service, there were no witnesses around. Just my family and Pastor West.

And not an hour later, my father walked back out of the church with the vigor of a man completely healed. Not only healed, but restored to the same strength he used to have before the cancer ever took hold of his lung.

How do you talk about that to the neighbors? How do you explain it without sounding like you're making it up?

We found that we couldn't. Not in a small town like that. Even though almost everyone went to the same church, there was a difference between going to church and actually believing.

Not just believing. *Knowing.* My parents and sister and I crossed some sort of bridge that day and found it was impossible to go back.

We only stayed in Macon for a few more months after that. Then my father took a job in Kansas City, where no one had ever heard of us.

Dr. Proul had his three-level protocol. But what we had just experienced was level number four. Or maybe even five.

Projecting. Assuming. Inviting. All of those depended on a certain amount of belief—or at least a temporary suspension of disbelief. As scientists, especially those of us who specialize in the theoretical, we have to be willing to imagine. To think, *Well, maybe this could be true. Let's find out.*

And sometimes that leads to the fourth level. *Believing.* Realizing intellectually that something is not only possible, but actually true. You might not have personal experience with it, but you can believe other people's accounts. You don't scoff at it and dismiss it.

You say yes, I believe you have extrasensory abilities. I don't have them myself, but I believe they exist. Yes, I believe you healed someone with the laying-on of hands. I accept intellectually that that could happen. Yes, I believe that aliens are real and they have visited us on Earth. I have read and heard too many accounts by people whose integrity and intelligence make them reliable witnesses— people like Dr. Jorge Diaz. A reliable scientist, not a kook. So intellectually, I accept all of those. Meaning I am willing to look at the evidence.

I think maybe a lot of the scientists in the group were at that level before the extraordinary events of the night. Maybe even poor Claudette had already accepted the theory of aliens, but seeing a spaceship in person was too much for her mind, at least at first. Then she, too, came around. Came to the fifth level: *Knowing.*

Knowing is hard. Even when you see the truth with your own eyes. It makes you give up your comfy, safe ideas. It challenges your lifelong view of how the world is, how things work, and what is possible even if it defies logic and sense and science.

A lot of people who might claim they believe in certain concepts rebel when it comes to that last step of *knowing* something magical or mystical is real. I saw it as my parents' former friends started to distance themselves after my father's healing.

They didn't want to see my dad playing touch football with his daughters in the back yard. They didn't want to see him standing upright and healthy as he strode around town.

They could only take it if he was still slowly dying. That was the reality they understood. But a complete healing? They couldn't accept it. Even though all of them might claim to be people of faith, my father's sudden cure scared the living daylights out of them.

A lot had just happened, out in that cold and snowy darkness. How were the scientists who had witnessed it explaining it to their scientific minds right now? Did they believe? Did they *know,* the way I did? I was suddenly very curious to find out.

As Dr. Proul, Jorge, Sheila, and I headed back along the snowy path toward the lights of the house, I had a theory about what we would find there. How the scientists would greet us, especially the miraculously healed Dr. Proul.

I enjoy the mental exercise sometimes of mapping out a whole theory and then seeing how close I come to the real answer whenever I find it.

It was how I kept going on my Pure Dark Energy project for so many difficult years. I would imagine the smaller steps all along the way—sometimes as small as wondering if two numbers in a math equation were correct—and those small, measurable victories gave me the energy and the will to keep going. Until one day I knew I had created what I heard about so many years before in that dark movie theater on a Saturday night.

I guessed that a certain number of the thirteen who had been with us were right now already packing to leave.

They might not want to try to drive on the snowy, twisty roads at night, but come first light, a good number of them would be gone.

I theorized that Bob was somewhere out of sight, maybe in his bedroom, but still under the impromptu guard. But those men who had tackled him would get tired of feeling responsible fairly soon. They'd want someone else, maybe a sheriff, to show up and take over the job.

The people who would be waiting for us on the first floor, in the main meeting space, would be the scientists who decided not to come with us out into the snow. There had been three of them: Bob, already taken care of (whatever that meant), and also the airplane engineer from Seattle and the woman who taught physics at Pepperdine.

They would have heard people talking when they returned, and now they wanted to know more. Natural human tendency. They had missed out on something that turned out to be highly dramatic. Now that it was just a story to them, they would hunger to know everything.

But there would be a few—I theorized maybe only three or four—who would be waiting with honest excitement to know what would come next. They had gone out willingly with the rest of the group, and now they were more curious than ever about what it all meant.

As we walked up the steps to the house, I pulled Sheila back by the sleeve. I wanted her to wait with me. As some kind of witness.

I couldn't help sharing my estimates with her. I wanted someone else to know whether I came close or not. Maybe it was ego, or just wanting some connection with someone who had just been through the same thing I had.

"I think there will be five people in the room when we walk in." I named the airplane designer, the woman from Pepperdine, and three others.

Sheila thought about it for a moment, then placed her own bet. "Only three people, but I don't know which ones."

We were both wrong. Bob was sitting in one of the wide, comfy chairs, scowling at everyone else to cover what I could see was fear.

His guards were gone. Maybe they had already gone up to their rooms to pack. They had done and seen enough. They were leaving first thing.

Claudette was there, looking flushed and bright eyed. For someone who had been hysterical earlier at the first sight of an actual alien spaceship, she was looking surprisingly together. She sat up eagerly in her chair and stared at Dr. Proul and the dried blood on his neck. But she seemed excited, not in the least bit upset.

There were three more women spread around the room in the chairs they had occupied earlier in the day.

And three men, for a total of seven scientists, not counting Bob the gun-crazy chemist. I wasn't counting Bob for anything. I wished he was already gone.

The plane designer and the woman from Pepperdine weren't there. Maybe they had heard about the story and escaped back to their rooms.

That made ten of us in all, out of the sixteen who had come to the conference.

Far more than I expected. But Dr. Proul didn't seem surprised.

"Let me wash up," he said. "But then I think we should talk about tonight. I know you're probably tired—"

"You think any of us are sleeping?" Claudette asked, almost with a note of humor in her voice.

Dr. Proul smiled. "All right. Just give me a few minutes."

Sheila leaned over to me and murmured, "Wine?"

I was tempted, but I wanted a clear head.

The two of us went up to the second floor kitchen, where I started a fresh pot of coffee. Just the smell of it brought me back down to earth. There was no one else in the kitchen, but Sheila and I still didn't speak. It was as if we both wanted to save it for when Dr. Proul came back.

Sheila seemed somber. Or maybe just pensive. It was hard to read her mood. Before long we heard Dr. Proul's footsteps on the wide log stairs and we left the kitchen to join him. He had washed off the blood from his neck and changed into a white T-shirt I could see poking out of the top of his black quarter-zip sweater.

"Anything we need to discuss?" Dr. Proul asked Sheila.

"Not a thing," she said.

I waited for him to ask me the same question or something else, but he kept on trotting down the stairs ahead of us back to the first floor. His vigor reminded me of my father. The renewed energy of a man brought back from the dead.

Dr. Proul took his position again at the front of the meeting room. He made eye contact with each person in turn, including Bob, who I saw look away. No shame in that one. He should be on his knees, begging his forgiveness for almost killing Dr. Proul. But people like Bob the chemist just get meaner and more aggressive the more they know they're wrong. I turned my head to keep Bob out of my periphery. He was dead to me.

Dr. Proul took in a breath. Then he smiled at the assembled group. "You probably expect me to ask you not to tell a soul outside this house what happened tonight. But quite the opposite. I hope you will."

4

"Let us review," said Dr. Proul. "Please, everyone. Tell me exactly what you saw tonight."

No one seemed especially eager to begin the discussion. So I plunged in.

"You faced north and held your arms up to the night sky. Then Dr. Diaz joined you. Then I did. Then the rest of the group joined in."

"I saw the glowing ball," Claudette said. "I … wasn't prepared to see anything. Even though you and Jorge had talked about aliens. I just wasn't prepared. I'm sorry, but I freaked out."

"No need to apologize," said Dr. Proul. "You aren't the first to react with fear. Is she, Bob?"

Dr. Proul turned to his would-be killer and stared at him with a bland look. Bob responded as one might expect, by muttering a few coarse expletives.

"At what point did you join us outside?" Dr. Proul asked him. "How much did you see?"

"Enough," Bob said. He folded his arms over his pouched belly and visibly clamped his mouth shut. Like a toddler threatening to hold his breath unless he got his way.

The front door of the mountain house opened. In walked two men I had never seen before. They wore black wool overcoats, heavy dark pants, and black boots they didn't bother taking off at the door, even though they were covered in snow. One was tall, maybe six-foot-something, with short blond hair I could see poking out of the bottom of his black wool hat. The second man was shorter, stockier, with brown hair and round cheeks that were rosy from the cold.

The two men didn't ask any questions, didn't ask which one was Bob, they simply walked straight to him and motioned for him to stand.

"What for?" he demanded. His eyes were wide with fright. "Who are you? I'm not going with you."

The taller stranger said, "You're under arrest for the attempted murder of Adam Proul."

"I wasn't aiming at him!" Bob the chemist shouted. "Tell them!" he told Dr. Proul. "I was aiming at that ... *thing*, and you know it!"

I noticed that neither man had shown any kind of identification. I'd watched enough police shows in my life span to know you're supposed to flash your badge and state your name. *Detective Jones. Officer Smith.* But the men just stood uncomfortably close to Bob the chemist and waited for him to come on his own power.

One tick, two … and the men had waited long enough. They each grabbed an arm and pulled Bob from his nice comfy chair. He started struggling. The rest of us in the room just watched in a mix of horror and also righteous vindication. What the two men said was true: Bob the gun-nut had shot Dr. Proul in the neck. And his victim would be dead out there in the snow right now, if not for other extraordinary events.

No one rose to Bob's defense. In fact, no one rose at all. We sat frozen in our chairs, watching the whole interaction unfold.

Bob the overweight chemist was no match for the two burly men who came for him. They bustled him out of the house with very little effort.

The snowy footsteps from their boots still dotted the glossy wooden floor. Some of the muddy ice was already starting to melt. It was going to leave a mess.

I listened for the sound of a car starting up. I didn't hear it. Maybe the house was too well-insulated to hear noise from outside. But it added to the mystery of the two men in black overcoats. They had arrived without warning and left as silently as they came.

Sheila turned in her chair to glance back at me. I shook my head slightly and shrugged. I didn't know what any of us were supposed to do. We were all following Dr. Proul's lead, and he still stood leaning against a table at the front waiting for the strangers to close the door behind them.

"What … what will happen to him?" Claudette asked.

"I image he'll be questioned," Dr. Proul said. "Everything will be fine. Don't worry. Now let's return to our discussion. I want to hear from all of you. What did you see tonight? What did you feel?"

It took a little while for us to warm to the discussion again, but eventually, despite the accumulated stress and the late hour, we enthusiastically recounted everything we experienced, moment to moment. Comparing observations, the way we scientists were trained to do. But also, as Dr. Proul asked, discussing how we felt about all of it—something scientists are rarely encouraged to share.

It was past one in the morning when we had finally talked ourselves to exhaustion. A few of the scientists were in my age group, and they must have been feeling as completely worn out as I was. The coffee I had had a few hours before had long ago lost its power. Looking around I could see drooping eyes. Slack faces. Frequent and robust yawns.

Dr. Proul could obviously see it all, too. "I think it's time to call it a night," he told us. "But I have just one more question for you first. You have all experienced the effect of Inviting. We called to an outer species, and it came. Forget the bad part." Dr. Proul dismissed the shooting and his near death and Bob's abrupt arrest all with a wave of his hand. "My question for you is, would you do it again? *Will* you do it again? We have three more nights together. We can still accomplish a great many things together, if you're still willing."

A silence moved among us, almost the same as the way the green alien light had woven among our stationary bodies. Sheila looked back at me again. I nodded. She smiled slightly and returned the nod.

One by one, we all voiced our agreement. Yes, we would do it again.

We were scientists. We were human. The urge to know is a palpable force.

"All right," said Dr. Proul. "Then get some sleep. Tomorrow we'll begin a more formal level of training. Thank you for your courage. Thank you for welcoming the future. I hope each of you will see how your own work plays a part in this future we can build together. Good night."

And with that, he strode off through the room and up the stairs and left us to puzzle through the implications of what he had said.

I saw the application to my own work immediately. I saw it when I first laid eyes on the alien ship. There were no visible engines—how could there be, when it first presented as a glowing orange sphere? It grew in place and became the large craft we eventually saw. There were no engines on that, either. No visible means of powering it.

Of course I took that all in and thought about myself.

It took years and years, but I finally discovered how to harness the Pure Dark Energy all around us. I could imagine a more advanced species learning that centuries— maybe even millennia—ago. If there were some way of finding out … of course I was eager to get another look at that ship and examine it more closely.

I looked around the room at the group of scientists who remained. Several physicists, an aerospace engineer, one evolutionary biologist, and Sheila, a specialist in telecommunications. Why was this the right time for all of our work? I thought about that discussion from earlier in the day.

Dr. Proul must have known back then what we would see in the dark night sky a few hours later. He must have known that our Inviting would land that big extraterrestrial fish.

How did the appearance of that alien ship intersect with my own and the other scientists' work? Why were we here? Why *us*?

As the two of us wearily climbed up the stairs to our respective third-floor bedrooms, I asked Sheila for her opinion.

"Does tonight change anything about your work?"

Sheila chuckled softly. "More than you can imagine. Yes. Definitely. What about you?"

"I want to see that ship again," I said. "If I thought it would come back tonight, I would go out there right now. Even though I'm about ready to fall asleep on my feet."

"What do you think about Bob?" Sheila asked.

"Good riddance," I said. Although the truth was I felt a little uneasy being so cold. I couldn't forget the look of fear on his face as the two dark-clad men hauled him out of the house. I don't care for violence. Despite what Bob did, I hoped they didn't hurt him. Lock him up somewhere, fine. But beat him or injure him, I didn't want to think about that.

"Who do you think those men were?" I asked. "They looked like federal agents to me. Not like rural cops at all."

Sheila yawned. "No idea. Good night, Angela. Been quite a day."

I returned to my room and took a hot shower. I changed into a flannel nightgown and thick wool socks. I should have passed out the minute I hit the bed, but I was too wound up to sleep.

I thought about writing in my notebook, but I had already talked about it too much. Writing it was more than I could bear at the moment, even though I knew I would want to make meticulous notes later, probably in the morning.

Instead I went to my window. It looked out on the north sky, where the ship had first appeared. I stared at the black night and the winking stars. Then despite the cold, I pushed up the lower half of the double-sash window.

The air was winter brisk, but at least there was no wind. I should have taken a moment to put on my ski coat over my nightgown, but I didn't want to take the time.

I leaned out into the darkness and held my arms wide, the way I had done before. Inviting. Luring. Asking it to come. I stood for a long time that way, just hoping.

But my ship didn't come. Maybe it didn't see me. Maybe I alone wasn't enough to tempt it without Dr. Proul standing by my side.

But by the next night I understood more. By the next night I could call it to me if I wanted.

And that began two of the best, most thrilling, nights of my life.

Followed by the worst.

5

I awoke on day two of the conference with the sun streaming in through my bedroom window, late, sometime after eight. I could still feel the accumulated exhaustion from the night before. I lay in bed for a while replaying everything in my head.

Something that stuck out. I hadn't really focused on it the night before, but now I realized how strange it was.

In all the discussion with Dr. Proul and the other scientists late last night, no one wanted to linger very long on the actual healing.

Including me. I glossed over it. Everyone else did, too. No one asked me how I did it. How it felt. How I knew to try.

It was as if they all took it for granted that one of us, not even necessarily me, would kneel by the dying Dr. Proul and place a hand on his mortal wound, and somehow by the grace of the alien force around us, the aliens' friend would be healed.

Even Jorge Diaz, the evolutionary biologist, didn't seem particularly curious.

But I was. As I lay in bed, I decided to go through it all again. Every moment, from my first impulse to take off my glove and place my hand against Dr. Proul's neck, to the sensation of smooth warmth as whatever power the green light had given me now flowed out of my heart and lungs, through my arm, and out from my hand into the exposed wound.

I thought about how I felt when I saw Dr. Proul sit up. I remembered Bob the chemist being so shocked, he vomited into the snow.

But I wasn't shocked. Pleased, yes. But not overjoyed or elated. Just … satisfied, I suppose.

And that felt strange in retrospect. It wasn't as if I had ever healed someone before. When Pastor West healed my father, I started bawling. Granted, I was very young, but still. I felt it deeply.

But now that I thought about it, Pastor West didn't seem overly moved by what he had done. Pleased, yes. Who wouldn't be? It was a job well done. But he didn't tear up or cry out, not even *Praise the Lord!* He accepted my father's enthusiastic handshake. Then he sent us on our way, out of the church.

He, like Dr. Proul, encouraged us to tell others what had happened. But my family learned very quickly that no one really wanted to hear.

And it was the same last night. I had a story to tell, if

anyone wanted to hear it. I could have described in intimate detail what it felt like to act as a conduit for the alien energy that flowed into Dr. Proul.

But I had seen behavior like that before. When I tried to describe to other scientists how my discovery of Pure Dark Energy was going to change the world. No more dependency on gas or oil or coal. No need for nuclear power plants or even solar or wind farms.

And because a rising tide lifts all boats, it would bring equity to the poorest places on Earth. People in small villages in remote places on the globe would no longer have to suffer without heat in their homes and power to pump and purify their water. They would have lights so they could cook and study at night. I could see it all—just like Dr. Proul said. I was projecting myself into a certain kind of future. A future made better by my own discovery.

And for years, I could nearly cry in frustration over the lukewarm reaction at best, scornful and cynical reaction at worst, of my peers in the scientific community. I thought it must be in how I was explaining it at conferences and writing about it papers I tried to get published. I thought I wasn't telling it right. If I was, surely everyone in the world would be as excited about it as I was.

And then, somewhere around ten years ago, I finally started to get a clue. It wasn't because I wasn't explaining it well enough. People understood, they just couldn't accept it.

It defied everything they believed about how energy on this planet worked. They didn't want to change those comfortable, core beliefs. How much of their science would have to be rewritten if they did? It's like physicists who dare to say that Albert Einstein wasn't exactly right. A whole respected history of scientific thought would have to be scrapped. No one except the most radical could even contemplate doing it.

So when I talked about energy that was free, that was all around us for the taking, that could be harnessed by anyone in the world and at very little cost—no wonder some of my colleagues were actually angry at what I suggested. I was cutting away at the core of what they believed.

And that, I realized as I lay in bed in Dr. Proul's mountain mansion, was the same way the scientists from last night were treating the miraculous healing they witnessed.

Maybe none of them were angry about it, but they didn't want to have to hear what happened in too great of detail.

It was already too much to accept that an alien ship had appeared. And then to have to accept that an alien light had moved among us all and touched our offered hands.

It made sense that Bob the chemist had vomited at the sight of Dr. Proul sitting up. It was too much. Circuits overloaded. Won't compute.

I could hear footsteps creaking on the polished oak floor of the third floor. People were up. I could hear them descending the stairs.

I got up and dressed and brushed my teeth and splashed cold water on my face. I was ready for coffee and for the breakfast I could smell through the crack under my door.

I joined the others in the second floor dining area. I

made a quick count: still the same ten from our debriefing the night before.

Still missing: Bob the chemist, of course, and the woman from Pepperdine. Also the plane engineer from Seattle.

And I didn't see the two men who had tackled Bob in the dark last night when the shot rang out, and then guarded him as they escorted him back to the house. In fact, I couldn't even remember which scientists they were. Maybe one had been from Purdue, but I wasn't sure. I couldn't remember who the sixteenth scientist was, either, or whether it was a man or a woman.

But it didn't really matter. Those of us who had decided to stay were part of an elite group now, as far as I was concerned.

Dr. Proul had promised to train us to make the most of what we hoped would be another alien interaction tonight. The other scientists and I prepared ourselves for the intensive learning with copious amounts of coffee and custom omelets prepared by the private chefs and toast and danishes and delicious selections of fruit.

A chime sounded from downstairs.

All conversation stopped. We all looked at each other.

I could feel everyone's nerves. We weren't sure what to expect. And yet the ten of us had all stayed on because we wanted to know.

We found our same chairs again on the first floor. The empty chairs interspersed among us served as some emblem that we were the brave ones.

I won't go through all of Dr. Proul's training. It was

both technical and emotional. Like a therapy session that explored the boundaries of our thinking, and then challenged us to push against our lifelong mental limits and start accepting something radically new.

I could see the fear on some of the other scientists' faces at times. One of the older men covered his face with a visibly shaking hand. Sheila turned in her chair several times throughout the day to check my reaction to something Dr. Proul had just said. We widened our eyes at each other and then returned to furiously writing our notes.

There was a long break after lunch so that people could nap or take a walk. Dr. Proul understood that our brains were running at full capacity and we needed time to adjust to everything we had heard.

The February afternoon light began fading by four o'clock. Which meant that darkness would be coming soon enough.

We had one more session before dinner. A chance for everyone to ask whatever questions they still had.

Dr. Jorge Diaz spoke up. "How will we know what they want?"

"You will know," Dr. Proul assured him.

"You said that before," Jorge said, "but pardon me for asking again. It's only that … I have been in situations when I have been face to face with our gray friends, and all I could do was smile and gesture and hope they understood they were welcome. But what I saw last night was different. I never saw a ship or an alien like that before. I don't feel I will know how to communicate with them, despite everything you've taught us today."

There was a murmur among the other scientists. Apparently Jorge spoke for a lot of them. For me, too. I was ready to get out and try—but how did I know I could really do it? If the opportunity came, as I dearly hoped it would, could I, a human, really connect with an advanced alien presence and do all that Dr. Proul had been encouraging us to do?

Dr. Proul leaned back against the small table behind him and took a moment before he answered. He must have been tired from holding the floor all day long. His voice was showing signs of overuse.

"When I was a boy," he said, "our family had an Australian Shepherd. Smartest dog I've ever known. My parents used to joke that Bounder could rewire our whole house while we were gone if we didn't give him enough jobs to occupy his mind.

"So my brother and I, just for fun, just as a weird project, came up with a long list of duties for Bounder to do every day while we were at school. Things like check all the doors to make sure they were closed and locked, pick up any dirty clothes any of us left on the floor—that sort of thing.

"I even wrote down the list and put it up on our fridge with a magnet, low on the door where Bounder could see it." Dr. Proul smiled. "As if he could read. But I was only eleven or twelve, and I had no inhibitions about what was and wasn't possible. Those kinds of things don't seem to grab us until we're teenagers, don't you think?"

A lot of us smiled in response. He was right. I didn't start worrying what people thought of my brilliant/crazy ideas until I was a freshman in high school. Then just like with the facts about my father's healing, I learned to suppress what I thought I knew. It was easier to fit in if I was average.

"Then one day when I got home from school," Dr. Proul said, "Bounder was waiting for me by the door, wagging his tail in a nervous kind of way. As if he had done something bad and knew he was in trouble. You know how dogs show that. They have terrible poker faces.

"But I loved the dog and always treated him like a buddy. I asked him what was wrong, and to show me. I said he wasn't in trouble, let's go figure this out.

"There was a dead bird in our back laundry area. I have no idea how it got in. All the windows in our house had screens.

"Bounder whined and pushed on the bird's stiff body with his nose. I think it was a sparrow. One of those common gray birds you see everywhere, so you don't pay attention.

"'What happened, boy?'" I asked him. Bounder whimpered and backed up. Agitated, clearly. But I could tell he wanted me to follow him.

"He took me to his water bowl. Now keep in mind, Bounder was a very tidy dog. He was long past tipping over his food bowl or his water. That was for his puppy stage, and he was a full-grown adult.

"But his water bowl was lying upside down. There was still a little leftover dampness on the tile floor. I righted the bowl and saw pressed into the bottom of it a small gray feather. I knew where that had come from.

"And then..." Dr. Proul sighed. But a kind of delight lit up his face. "I saw it all. Bounder sent it to me as one complete package, into my mind. He showed me the whole story of what had happened.

"I knew I didn't imagine it, because my imagination wasn't that inventive. The information came into my mind from the dog, I have no doubt. Here is what he told me.

"When all of us left for the day, my brother and I went first to catch the bus. Then my father and mother took off to work, but my father forgot something and had to come back.

"In his hurry, he left the front door open while he looked for whatever he'd forgotten. And a bird flew in. I have no idea why. That wasn't normal bird behavior.

"My father didn't notice it, and soon he ran out the door again and shut the bird inside our house.

"Bounder had already completed the first task on his list, to check that all the doors were closed and locked, but now he had to start over again. He didn't mind, he told me in this story he passed wholly into my mind. He began his routine again, trotting from door to door to door, and that's when he discovered the little gray bird flitting itself frantically against our living room window.

"It was upsetting. Bounder didn't know what to do. He was a shepherd, not a bird dog, so his instincts didn't include chasing the bird down and carrying it around in his mouth.

"The bird tried other ways of getting out. Throwing himself against different windows.

"At some point the bird was just exhausted. And that was when Bounder's gentle ways came into play.

"He convinced the bird to come get a drink. Don't ask me how. Can dogs and birds communicate? Not with barks and tweets, but maybe telepathically, between species? I have no idea," said Dr. Proul. He seemed frustrated by that hole in his general knowledge.

I was sitting forward on my comfy wide chair, fascinated about where this was going. I thought I knew, but I didn't. Dr. Proul went on.

"However he convinced it, the bird did in fact come to Bounder's water bowl and perch on the edge of it and take little sips. I could see it in Bounder's memory ball. That's what I've come to think of it as. Then Bounder ... again, let me say what a gentle and wonderful dog he was. But he took the bird in his mouth and crunched down, and dumped the bird in the water.

"And Bounder stood there for a minute or two watching the bird float. Then he hit the bowl with his paw and dumped the bird and the water on the floor.

"He picked up the bird in his mouth and carried it gently into the laundry room. He laid it on the floor, just where Bounder showed me when I got home from school. And the dog was upset about it. I could feel him asking me in his memory ball, *Did I do right? Am I in trouble?* I just stood there looking at the whole situation and seeing it from Bounder's perspective, and I had no idea what to think or say.

"I scratched him behind the ears. 'It's okay, boy. I'll take care of it now.' I got a paper towel from the kitchen and came back and picked up the dead bird and carried it outside, thinking I might bury it.

"Or maybe just throw it in our outside garbage can. I stood there holding the bird while Bounder stared up at me with his mismatched eyes, one an eerie ice blue and the other a deep brown, and he looked at me like I was some hero come to save the day. Hardly.

"Outside under the crab apple tree in our front yard, I found three more dead birds. All the same species as the bird in my hand. Bounder saw them, too, and whined.

"I went to the garage to get my dad's shovel. I wasn't about to start picking up all the others just with my hands.

"On the way to the garage I found two more dead birds. It was insane. Like a Hitchcock movie."

"So what was it?" Claudette asked. "What happened? Some kind of disease?"

"Pesticide," Dr. Proul said. "Our neighbor had blanketed his lawn with it. Some of it must have drifted over to our yard and coated the apples and the tree. Maybe the birds ate the apples, or maybe the pesticide just got in through their skin. I don't really know. But the bird that got into our house was already sick, I think. And what's more, I think Bounder knew it, too."

"So, what," one of the men asked. "It was a mercy killing?"

"Not exactly," said Dr. Proul. "At least not how Bounder told me in the memory ball he sent to my mind.

"It was one of his duties, the last one on the list I had made up for him, in big handwritten letters: PROTECT

OUR HOME. I was just a kid, messing around, thinking up duties for our family dog.

"I'm not saying Bounder could read it—I'm not going that far," said Dr. Proul with a smile, "but there's no question in my mind that Bounder knew what we wanted and expected from him. He was a guard dog, after all, that breed. He evolved to come up with ingenious solutions to whatever dangers were threatening the flock.

"So a bird got in and was acting strangely, and the dog knew something was wrong. He couldn't chase it around in the air, but he somehow lured it down to the ground where it would perch on his water bowl. Then you know the rest."

Dr. Proul looked around at the group. I think he wanted someone else besides him to say it.

So I did. "This is your long answer to Jorge's question, isn't it? We don't have to worry about communication with another species. We don't have to understand the same language. The information will get to us anyway."

"It will get to you anyway," Dr. Proul confirmed. "Trust that. You'll see for yourselves tonight. When another species wants to communicate with us, they find a way. Whether it's with a memory ball or however you'll come to think of it. I have seen it in action for myself for at least the last ten years. But you're all scientists, and you need to discover it for yourselves. Verify it. You will. I have no doubt of that.

"We'll meet back here once it's fully dark. Grab some dinner. Take a rest. We have a lot to do tonight."

At seven o'clock the ten of us and Dr. Proul gathered

again outside the house on the round flat area of cleared snow. Those who hadn't dressed warmly enough the night before had done better this time, although I could see that Sheila still wore her thin leather gloves and still had to clap them together frequently to keep her hands from freezing.

"Ready?" Dr. Proul asked. I was. I think we all were. We stood together and raised our arms to the dark night sky in a sign of welcome. Inviting the ship once again.

It did come. And this time it brought three more ships with it.

6

The ship presented once again as a glowing orange-red sphere at first. It retained its shape and size until it was close enough that someone could have hit it with a well-aimed baseball—or a bullet.

Then three silver-white glowing spheres came out of it. If the orange ship was a basketball, these were softball-sized. All four ships came to rest above our heads and began expanding. The orange sphere grew into a triangle shape, as it did the night before, and grew to loom over our patch of snow. Maybe it was a trick of my eyes, but I thought it looked smaller than it did the previous night. The silver-white globes retained their spherical shapes and expanded to the size of VW Bugs.

We all still stood with our arms upraised. My muscles were starting to tire, but I didn't dare lower my arms—not if this was my first way of communicating that our friends were welcome.

But then Dr. Proul told us quietly that we could relax and just wait. The aliens would take it from here.

And just as it did the night before, a bright green light exited from the larger ship and began swimming among the scientists.

But I was watching the silver-white globes. They were new, so they had my full attention. It's funny how quickly we become accustomed to the extraordinary. I had already seen and felt the green light. I didn't even hold out my hand this time to touch it.

Smaller shapes began breaking off from the silver-white globes. They floated down to us until they hovered about a foot above our heads. Then they resolved into new, humanoid shapes. Like beings of light with a head and two arms, but no legs. Instead their bodies tapered off at the bottom like the end of a seed pod, like an okra. But with a slight curve to the ends, like a comma.

The beings floated down lower as they grew in size. Once they were about three feet tall, they held their positions waist-high to each of us in the group. Eleven scientists, including Dr. Proul, and eleven glowing beings paired with each of us. Like alien dance partners assigned to their humans.

The glowing being at my side moved in front of me and filled my field of vision. I knew there were other things going on all around me, but I couldn't look anywhere but into the spectacular shape before me.

It was neither male nor female. Not that I could see. It had no facial features. No eyes or nose or mouth. Its skin, if that's what it was, was translucent, and I could see a silvery-white light glowing from inside it, shimmering whenever it moved in the cold night air.

There was a different colored light, a pale rose-orange, glowing inside its head and the top of its chest. That was what drew my eyes. I felt I was gazing at the creature's beautiful face, even though there were no eyes gazing back at me.

The light coming from the creature was both soft and bright. It felt soothing to look at, almost as though there were a protective liquid gel over my eyeballs filtering out any harsher light. It was not like staring into a light bulb or a flickering flame. The light felt cool, not hot. I never felt as though I needed to look away to preserve my vision.

The creature's hands were shaped like mittens, with only the thumb a distinct separate digit. The arms were stubby and wide, more like the early stages of wings you see on newly-hatched baby birds.

The closest comparison I can make is to the aquatic creature called a sea angel. Their bodies are shaped like okra pods, too, with comma-shaped tails, and they have what look like small translucent wings coming off of their shoulders. But the sea angels have two soft-looking horns at the top of their heads. The alien before me had a smooth, round dome of a head, with the rose-orange light glowing out of the center.

If this all sounds too strange to be beautiful, then I am not doing the creature justice. It was exquisite. So beautiful I wanted to cry. It conveyed to me an all-encompassing feeling of tranquility and love. I have never felt so at peace in my life.

Dr. Proul had instructed us to speak to the aliens. To introduce ourselves. So I did.

"I am Dr. Angela Corliss," I whispered, feeling only slightly foolish. Or not really foolish, so much as too forward. I wanted the creature to make the first move. I didn't want to startle it or somehow prove myself unworthy of contact by coming across as a brash American, all noise and bluster. I wanted to be quiet. Little. I wanted to match the floating alien's energy.

But I shouldn't have been afraid of the gentle creature's reaction. It wasn't afraid of me. It didn't suddenly spirit off into the air.

Instead it warmed me with the brighter glow from its face, as if I had blown on a fledgling fire and now the flames took hold of the tinder.

The way the alien's body was made, its arms and mitten-like hands splayed out from its upper chest and moved only slightly back and forth like fins. But somehow I got the idea to remove my gloves and reach out to those hands and match my palms against their surface.

Again, expecting the creature to flinch. To fly away. To show me I had gone too far.

And once again what I did seemed exactly the right thing after all. The creature pressed its surprisingly solid hands against my own. They were half the size of my own palms. Like playing patty-cake with a toddler.

The texture of its skin was warm with what felt like a liquid heat. Like a heating pad wrapped in a moist towel. Not clammy at all. The moisture seemed to conduct the heat into my palms with great efficiency.

To my right and left, elsewhere in the crowd, I could hear some of the other scientists making odd but clearly joyful kinds of sounds. *Ohs!* and *Yesses* and inarticulate hums. We sounded like the background choir of a soft choral hymn, taking the place of an organ or other loud instrument. The sound of our voices was all that was needed. We were the sound of crickets and tree frogs serenading the night.

My own voice vibrated inside my throat. After introducing myself, I ran out of things to say. So I stood with my boots braced against the snow, knees locked for no other reason than my nerves, and I kept my hands pressed gently against the glowing creature's mittens and wondered what came next. What was I supposed to do?

I thought of Dr. Proul assuring us we would know. So I let out a breath and saw it fog between the alien's face and my own. Then I drew the air back in and continued gazing into the creature's beautiful glowing light.

I heard a kind of *May I?* I only say it was kind of that, because human words can't do it justice. The alien was asking me for permission, but asking in such a way that my heart yearned for it, ached for it, yes, please, please don't delay. I didn't even know what it wanted, but whatever it was, I wanted it more than I could bear.

Then came what I can only describe as a melding.

I felt the creature slip past my hands, past my arms, and in through my solid chest.

It was no longer visible in front of me. It was *inside* me. I could feel it the same way I felt the green alien light from the night before filling me with a warm soothing energy. But the sea angel-like creature didn't just touch my hand and work from there. It stepped inside me and began growing.

I could feel it expanding through my chest cavity. A warm and liquid light. Then into my throat and up through my head. I wondered if anyone looking would see the alien's rose-orange glow seeping out through my eyes or the skin on my face.

Its short, stubby fin-like, wing-like arms pushed their way outward until the creature's inner hands filled my own to the fingertips.

Its tapered tail spread through my abdomen. I shifted my hands down to my hips and pressed them inward on my flesh to confirm the spreading heat was there.

Then its tail must have divided, like a tadpole sprouting legs, because I could feel the warmth swimming down both of my legs, into my boots, to the tips of my toes.

It all happened fairly quickly. In less time than it took me to describe it. And although reading it might frighten you or make you feel uncomfortable, inside the experience it felt as natural as drinking a glass of water and feeling it slake my thirst.

And then, the download.

The transfer of information.

The moment when my chosen dance partner proved he or she or it was the right match for me.

I can't call it learning. That sounds too step-by-step. Maybe it was more like what Dr. Proul described with his Australian Shepherd, Bounder.

I got it *all*. All in one giant ball of information. Connections I was missing and might never have found on my own for many more years.

Pure Dark Energy. I saw what it truly meant. I saw where it was, how to find it, how to use it, how to make the inventions that would allow me to use it.

I thought I already had all of that. In my pride, in my brashness. I had been working on it for over forty years. I had designed inventions of my own. I thought I was ready to share it. I was so frustrated that it was ready to go, but no one would listen to me.

I was so wrong. I wasn't ready at all. What I thought I knew was a child's picture book compared to a hundred-volume encyclopedia.

My gentle, glowing, beautiful teacher was filling me with the information I needed and probably wouldn't have been able to understand in the least if she/he/it had come to me with the same ball of total instruction back when I began my Pure Dark Energy journey.

I have come to believe in the magic of timing. I have come to see what Dr. Proul was asking us about on the first day of his conference: Why now? Why are we alive in these exact times?

As the alien filled me with the knowledge I needed, I understood that I was alive at exactly the right time, and an hour earlier or later would have meant I missed it.

I had been so absorbed in the experience I tuned out any sounds around me. But now, for whatever reason, they began flooding in.

The sounds of sobbing. Deep gut sobbing. Both by the

men and the women. My fellow scientists were absolutely overwhelmed.

My own joy was so overpowering, I couldn't muster a single tear. Instead I could hear a kind of moan forming inside the vibration in my throat. Like an animal who lacked the mechanism for speech, and so had to resort to yips and gurgles and groans.

When the lesson was over—if that is what it was—the alien creature gently began extracting itself from the contours of my body. I could feel the heat reversing course, first from the tips of my toes to my feet and calves and thighs, then area by area until it finally pulled itself all the way out and floated in front of me again, its stubby arms gently pulsing in the cold night wind as though it were underwater.

That was when I cried. I could feel tears slipping down my cheeks and instantly freezing. But I was smiling so broadly I ran out of room inside my cheeks.

It was the most moving, enlivening, mind-expanding experience I had ever had in my life. In a way it felt as though I had gone through a near-death experience the way I've heard them described. I could understand why some people felt so devastated to be sent back to their bodies and their ordinary lives. When you've tasted the celestial and the infinite, your old human existence feels as though you're crawling on your belly in the dirt.

I was panting for breath. I felt too overwhelmed. But at the same time, I could feel the incredible changes to my body and mind, and I wanted them. Wanted them so badly. I wouldn't turn them away for all the world.

The dance was over. All around me I could see other floating alien bodies begin to ascend toward the silvery-white globes that had transported them there.

A few of the scientists cried out. *No! Not yet! Come back!*

But I let mine go. Clinging wouldn't add another minute.

Eleven of us stood in the cold and the dark and watched as the lights of the spheres rose to a particular height, and then all shot off into the sky at the same time.

I sank to my knees. The snow felt good against my bare palms. I was still breathing too hard. I'm an old woman, after all.

My position must have seemed good to some of the others, because right and left several of them dropped to their hands and knees and heaved out their own breaths, all of us just trying to adjust to what had just happened.

"Is everyone all right?" Dr. Proul called out.

We answered with yesses and grunts and moans.

I could only assume that everyone else in the group had just received an infusion of what felt like infinite information about their own, specific work.

An infusion that could leap us all forward not just by years, but by decades.

What was this place? Who was Dr. Proul to bring this to us? Who were each of us to receive it?

It was a holy moment in my scientific life. It was grace mixed with knowledge mixed with magic.

Part of me felt frantic to run back to the house and begin writing everything down.

Part of me said *It's all right. You'll remember. It's part of you now.*

Dr. Proul said, "Let's go back inside. I need to get you all warm."

He was right. Now that the alien warmth had left my body, I could feel a deep cold invading my blood and my bones.

We stumbled, dazed, along the dark snowy path. No one spoke. We didn't have it to give.

At one point I felt someone squeeze my right forearm. I looked over and saw Sheila walking beside me. She met my eyes for a moment then continued walking past. But I saw enough of her enraptured expression to know that she was changed as much as I was. I almost didn't want to see any of my colleagues now in the light. I thought I might not be able to bear it. Like seeing someone higher than high on some kind of drug. It doesn't feel natural to witness what exceeds human limits.

Someone from Dr. Proul's staff, maybe the chefs from the second floor, had set out bottles of water beside every plush armchair.

I sank into the one I'd been occupying the past two days. I drank the bottle down. Everyone else drank theirs.

Dr. Proul gave us time. He didn't start in right away. He must have done this before, with other groups over the years, and he knew what the participants needed.

For myself, I needed a good long joyous scream. Something to scrub off the excess energy flooding my veins.

But I sat there like all of the other scientists and caught up with my breathing and caught up with my mind. It took fifteen or twenty minutes. Dr. Proul simply waited, during much of the time with closed eyes.

Then at some internal signal his eyes sprang open again, and the man smiled at us like someone who had just pulled off the greatest surprise.

"Not all at once," he said, but the side of his mouth quirked up, like he knew it was a joke. He knew we were all still too stunned to put any of it into words.

"Martin," he said, addressing the scientist sitting furthest back. "Let me start with this question: Did that solve a few things for you?"

Martin gripped the sides of his plush chair. He pulled himself forward, like someone launching themselves on their luge sled.

"Holy hell, Proul," he boomed in a voice louder than I'd ever heard him use. Then he added a few curse words. Then he smiled. "Where were you thirty years ago? You could have saved me a whole lot of trouble."

Other scientists murmured in agreement. Which told me they had all had the same experience I had. Learning in one ball of information what they had been striving to understand for years—for decades. And here it was, in a clearing outside this luxurious remote cabin.

But that's not right. It wasn't the place that made the difference. It was Dr. Proul learning how to invite them.

I suppose he could have done that anywhere. On a cliff somewhere in California. By a lake in Idaho.

Maybe I could do it, if I learned how. Maybe back home in Wisconsin I could open my window, lean out and open my arms, and invite in the same alien who had danced with me tonight.

But I could imagine that reaching that same level of expertise would take as long as I've already spent pursuing my theoretical physics.

You have to choose at some point. You can't do everything. You can't know and learn everything. You specialize. And then you try to learn from someone who knows what you need.

That man was obviously Dr. Adam Proul.

And I had a moment of secret pleasure, thinking about how I had saved his life the night before.

If not for that, none of us in that room would have had the experience we just had.

Why am I alive in these times? To save Dr. Proul's life and then press hands to hands with an alien lifeform who knew more about Pure Dark Energy than I did after forty years of study.

Where was Dr. Proul back then? I wasn't sure how old he was, but maybe forty years ago he was an eleven-year-old boy learning how to communicate with his dog.

You can't overthink these things. You'll drive yourself mad.

You just have to take what comes and go ahead and let it change you.

Once the preliminary cursing from Martin was over, people started wanting to talk about it. Eventually I did, too.

We stayed up until people were actually falling asleep

mid-sentence. Then we all forced ourselves to climb the Everest-seeming stairs.

My pal Sheila stumbled up the log steps beside me. She looked as wrung out as I felt.

"Thank you for saving his life last night," she said.

I was surprised, and also pleased, that she said it.

"I'll tell you a story tomorrow," I said, "about my father. I realize I've been around miracles all my life, and I eventually start acting like they're no big deal. But they are. Tonight was…"

I had already said it all. Everyone had said it all. Sheila simply answered, "Yeah."

I had just enough juice in me left to brush my teeth and change into my nightgown. I probably needed a hot shower, but the task felt too monumental.

I slept hard and woke even later than before. And I lay in bed once again and tried to organize my thoughts.

It was day three of the conference. We would all have to leave this place the day after tomorrow.

We had two more nights of splendor.

I couldn't imagine what else Dr. Proul would spring on us. I felt like I'd already received everything I could ever want or need.

But I was wrong, of course. The mind and heart always hunger for more. It's the essence of being a greedy human.

What would have happened if we stopped after night two? What would my life—all of our lives—have been if we had simply banked our gains and driven away?

Looking back is always dangerous. We must accept what we cannot change.

And despite everything that happened, I wouldn't give any of it back.

7

By the time I finally pried myself off the bed and took a hot shower and washed my hair and did all the normal parts of my routine as if nothing had changed, it was past ten o'clock. But Dr. Proul had already told us in the wee hours of the morning that we had a free day today. He was giving us time to absorb everything that we learned. We would reconvene after lunch, so that anyone could continue asking him what questions they had.

I thought I should have questions—a whole notebook full of them—but the truth was, I didn't. I felt mentally full. I assumed that every answer I wanted was somewhere contained now inside my mind. I just needed to take my time poking around in it, organizing it, seeing what all was there.

To that end, I was glad to have several hours now to myself to drink coffee, have a hot breakfast of oatmeal and brown sugar, and stare out the large clear windows of the mountain cabin as the snow gently fell.

Where we crossed each other's paths, my colleagues and I exchanged quiet, polite greetings, but otherwise we all kept to ourselves. I'm sure everyone still felt raw from the night before. We were all trying to acquaint ourselves with a new kind of reality. I can imagine it was harder for some of them than others. I was already acquainted with the miraculous, but I still found myself looking around the house and out the windows with a sense that all of the colors were brighter now. The shapes of things sharper. As though some filter had been removed and now I could see everything with more clarity.

After a while I poured myself a third mug of coffee and went back to sit in one of the comfy chairs on the second floor that looked out through the grand windows toward the west side of the house. There were patches of blue in the sky despite the falling snow. I hoped the blue would win out so we would have clear skies that night.

I was surprised to see down below two people out walking in the snow. From the shape and size of them, they appeared to be a man and woman. They wore heavy over-coats and serious-looking snow boots. They had dark wool caps underneath the hoods of their coats.

They did not turn left toward the front door. Instead they continued walking past the front of the house and the parking area where all of our rental cars sat covered in pillows of white. I craned my neck trying to see where they thought they were going, but I lost sight of them and soon gave up caring.

The scientist in me knew I needed to go write down what I learned the night before. So even though I was comfortable exactly where I was, I made myself get up and return to my room.

The house must have had a back entrance, although I hadn't seen it for myself. I never felt comfortable exploring in other people's houses. I stuck to the places where I'd been shown I could go.

The third floor had bedrooms both to the right and the left of the stairs. My room was a few doors to the right. Sheila's was two doors beyond mine. I had seen other scientists come and go from their rooms over the past two days.

I hadn't paid attention to where most of the people were sleeping. Some of them were on the second floor, too. It just didn't matter to me.

But now I was surprised to see the couple who emerged at the very end of the hallway down on the left. Surprised because they hadn't passed me on the stairs, but had come up some other way.

And surprised because I recognized the size and shape of the man and woman I had seen walking in the snow, even though they were no longer wearing their boots or heavy overcoats.

And most of all, surprised because they were two people I thought had already left the conference after the first night: the woman in her forties from Pepperdine, and the man in his early fifties who was the airplane engineer from Seattle.

Neither of them had come out with us to conduct the

first night's lesson in Inviting. They had stayed behind, just like Bob the gunslinger chemist.

When we all returned to the house after the big drama of Bob shooting at the sphere and hitting Dr. Proul instead, Pepperdine and Seattle were still noticeably absent. I assumed they had driven away, despite the darkness, or else were hiding in their rooms until they could safely leave in the morning.

And yet here they were.

Going in the same room together.

I wasn't sure if they saw me. I didn't hail to them and they didn't acknowledge me at all.

Why stay at a conference that you clearly didn't approve of? They had stopped coming to any of Dr. Proul's lectures and they hadn't come out with the group on either night.

The soap opera lover in me had a wicked theory. The two were lovers, here to meet up from their respective homes on opposite sides of the west coast. A little hanky panky under the guise of scientific advancement.

Then just the thought of it made me feel low and primitive all over again. As if I myself hadn't advanced one inch. Here I had spent my last two nights in the company of aliens from other worlds. That was where I wanted to keep my mind. I let myself back into my room and took out my notebook and made up for my momentary human lapse by writing up my notes for the next few hours.

I decided not to have lunch with everyone else. I waited until just before the afternoon session with Dr. Proul, and grabbed a few pieces of fruit from the second-floor kitchen on my way down the stairs. Another mug of rich coffee and I was good to go.

I was the last of our group to join the others back in the first-floor meeting room.

I could feel it almost the instant I stepped into the space. There was a strange, palpably depressed mood in the air.

Dr. Proul must have experienced it before—in fact, maybe every time before for as long as he had been running these conferences.

Because he addressed it head on. "You all feel deflated. It's natural. Don't be concerned."

"I feel sick," Claudette said. "I mean, physically ill. Like I have the flu."

There were murmurs of agreement throughout the room.

I sat in my customary chair and slipped out of my woolen clogs so I could sit with my feet tucked under me cross-legged. I leaned back into the cushions and cradled my coffee mug between my hands. I didn't feel like talking, but I was ready to watch the movie of whatever other people would do or say in this already strange session.

"Jorge?" Dr. Proul said. "Would you mind sharing with everyone what you told me earlier?"

The evolutionary biologist sat up in his chair near the front of the room and twisted around so we all could see him.

I was struck again by his distinctive hair. Thick brown locks with that stripe of gray down the right side. I wondered if he liked it or if it embarrassed him.

"There is a concept in evolution," Jorge told us, "about adjusting to gains. A species will suddenly advance in some dramatic way, but it doesn't stay there. It falls back a few steps. Maybe seems to forget what it learned. But it is a known resting period. Soon it will return to the new advancement, and continue on from there."

"Think of our first day," Dr. Proul said. "Our first lesson. Projecting. Last night you learned about entirely new levels in your own base of knowledge. It's natural to fall back, like Jorge said. To feel sick," he added, gesturing toward Claudette. "But this is temporary. We are all living organisms. We are not machines. A shock to the system affects us. But you'll see it affects you for the good. You'll pick up from a new spot much further along your path, and continue on from there. Is that what you were telling me, Jorge?"

"Yes," he said. "Not in those exact terms, but yes."

"So now what I'm suggesting," said Dr. Proul, "is that we repeat that first lesson, but now from this new place in your evolution. Understanding that what you all received last night was *meant* to help you leap ahead. Our friends are here to help us. They want us to catch up. They want to help us create a peaceful, advanced world. And maybe you understand now that everyone here in this room is alive now, in these times, to play a specific part in that.

"So come on, now," said Dr. Proul. "Let's spend some time projecting ourselves into *that* future."

I'll admit my heart did a double-time. I smiled. I heard some of the other scientists laugh. In all of my contemplation over the past several hours, I hadn't thought of it the way Dr. Proul was saying. But he was right. And Jorge was right. We had all taken a gigantic leap over the past two nights, and now we should be able to look into the future with completely fresh eyes.

That was what I had struggled with as I sat on my bed in my room upstairs and tried to make sense in my notes of what I was thinking and feeling.

Now I realized that all of my ideas about what was possible were no longer valid. Erase. Fresh board. Stop trying to fit my old life and my old ideas into this brand new container that had grown around me.

I could see that the others were starting to come around. Claudette drank some water from the bottle near her chair. She didn't look as pale and queasy as she had when she first spoke up a few minutes ago.

"What is the future *now*?" Dr. Proul asked us. "Now that all of you know so much more than you did before? What can you do with it? What can you make? What can you share? What can you teach us?"

I closed my eyes and felt that new future rushing in. Inventions. Possibilities. Solutions.

By the time the session was over, I couldn't wait for darkness to fall. Once it did, I practically skipped out across the new-fallen snow, ready to invite the spaceships and my alien dance partner and find out what more I could possibly receive.

The snow was still falling. Visibility was rough. I shielded my eyes with my hand and looked up into the sky.

The ten of us and Dr. Proul lifted our arms to the white-shrouded sky.

And then the air around us began to change.

It grew noticeably warmer. The snow no longer fell. The sound felt muffled. I assumed it was because of the thick fleece hat I wore low around my ears.

"My God," someone whispered. And I finally saw what was obvious.

The ship hadn't come to us as a sphere this time. It didn't hover above us over the snow. There were no silver-white globes accompanying it and growing into the size of VW Bugs.

The main ship was still large and triangular-shaped. It still seemed about twice as large as the clearing where we stood.

But this time the ship was all around us. Protecting us from the weather and the cold.

We were *inside* the ship. The ship had landed on Earth and somehow brought us all inside.

8

———————

A pale green light suffused the interior of the ship. I could see my fellow scientists in there with me, but not exactly. Everyone's bodies seemed to fade in and out of view. No, not in and out of view, in and out of *existence*. Materializing and de-materializing. I looked down at my arms, encased in several layers of warm clothing, and both the various fabrics and my skin were like pointillist art, just dots of yellow and white and green lights that would make up the painting of Angela Corliss if you looked at me from far away.

But that wasn't all. The air felt both pure and also dead. Pure to breathe in, even better than oxygen, but dead in that it sucked up all the sound.

I once gave an interview at a radio station—back in my days of trying to convince the world that Pure Dark Energy was the way of the future—and we conducted it inside a recording room with sound-deadening panels all along the walls. Every word the interviewer and I spoke seemed to fall from our mouths straight into a void. I listened to the interview later and it sounded professional and well-engineered, but the experience itself gave me the shivers. As if I had been cut off from the outside world and now existed down in some deep, bottomless hole—but a hole with no echo, no natural soundwaves at all. A dead place I couldn't wait to leave.

But despite the deadened noise, everything inside the ship felt alive. In fact—I know this will sound strange, but it came to me in another complete ball, just like the information from the alien the night before—I had the sense that the ship itself was living. It was not some mechanical wonder from a futuristic alien society. It was a sentient creature just as the aliens were. They lived together and flew together through space as partners, not as pilots and machine.

In this hazy, mysterious realm where my fellow scientists and I were only half visible, I was not afraid. I did not cower in place and wish I were somewhere else. I wanted to explore. I was curious. And I could see from the points of light making up my colleagues' faces that many of them felt the same way.

We began walking forward with our arms outstretched, as though we were trapped somewhere in the darkness and had to feel our way around. It was strange that we all reacted in that same way, reaching out to feel or to steady ourselves. I almost laughed at the sight. If this was some kind of experiment to test human behavior, all of us were demonstrating the same reaction at the same time.

But that wasn't true. I saw that Dr. Proul remained where he was at the edge of the group and seemed calm and peaceful. He must have done this countless times before. But for the rest of us, it was like walking for the first time on the moon.

I knew we were inside the sentient ship, but it wasn't because of any of the interior furnishings. There was no ship's bridge. No displays or controls. Not even any seating where the aliens we met the night before could rest their floating forms.

The floor was a kind of soft, golden metal. It held our weight without losing its form, but it was as comfortable as walking on thick carpet. The golden metal continued up about a quarter of the sides, then everything above it was clear, like a glass dome on top of the ship, with a full view all around us.

I could see delicate flakes of snow falling against the ship and instantly melting. It must be exuding the same kind of warmth on the exterior as it did inside.

I unzipped my ski coat. I would have taken it all the way off, but there wasn't any place to put it and I didn't want to just dump it in a heap.

A few of the others saw me unzip my coat, and they then did the same. But their coats were only dots of light anyway. Open or closed, they drifted in and out of sight just like the bodies inside them.

I realized then that even though what I saw were solid objects materializing and de-materializing every few seconds, my coat zipper felt normal and solid to me. I patted my right hand against my left arm. Solid and normal.

I wouldn't have done it with just anyone, but Sheila was standing close to me and I felt we were friendly enough that she wouldn't mind. I reached out and clasped her coat sleeve and the arm beneath it. Even though she faded in and out while I held onto her, I could feel her arm as if it remained fully solid.

Sheila met my gaze. She smiled. Then even though her lips were only half-formed to my eyes, I saw her say, "Watch this."

She bent her knees and pushed her boots off the golden floor. She floated upward. Gently and smoothly, until she caught the clear domed ceiling with her flattened palms. Then she pushed off and floated gently down to the floor. Of course I copied her the moment she landed.

Then all around me, except for Dr. Proul, scientists were floating and bobbing like children in a jumping castle. They were laughing. Giggling. Some of them whooping out loud. Their voices fell flat and dissipated as soon as they hit the air, but the mood was so different from the afternoon I could feel everyone's relief. I jumped off the floor several times myself. I could have done it all night. The feeling of free floating was addictive.

And then the light inside the ship changed from pale green to a beautiful white. Not harsh in any way, but instead soothing on my eyes. And the change of the light signaled that play time was over.

I was expecting—hoping—to see my alien dance partner from the night before. I felt I had barely spent enough time staring at the beautiful creature. I tried to draw it in my notebook, but failed utterly. I might as well have been drawing a stick figure for how close I got to the real thing.

The aliens with the mitten-shaped hands were not our companions this time.

Instead a new species of alien came to us like tall thin pillars of pale yellow light interspersed among the dots that made up the human forms, including me.

The beams of light were maybe a foot in diameter, and reached from the floor all the way up to the domed ceiling. Then they began to take shape. First reducing their height until they were all about six feet tall, then forming oblong-shaped heads and long spindly arms and long legs, each of which had either three long fingers or three long toes.

Their eyes were oblong-shaped, too, and tilted to the sides. The eyes were proportionate to the aliens' heads, and almost entirely black inside, with just a thin rim of dark brown encircling the large pupils.

I didn't see any sign of a nose or ears. Their mouths were very short and thin, more like slits than lips.

And though once again I may not have done an alien creature justice with my description, I can attest that these tall, thin yellowish aliens were majestic and beautiful. The way they moved was so graceful and fluid, they seemed to be both made of water and living inside it.

Having met an entirely different species the night before, I found I was staring in awe at these new ones and felt completely without fear. As if I could meet a new species every night from now on, and it was already starting to feel natural and not bizarre in the least.

There were eight of them inside the ship with us. All of them looked exactly the same to my eyes, but I grant there were probably differences. Maybe the shade of yellow on one of them was paler than another. Maybe their body shapes looked distinctly different to each other.

The alien closest to the center of the ship held out its three-fingered hand in a welcoming gesture. And even though its mouth wasn't large enough to manage a smile, I still thought I saw it.

There were no words expressed. I doubt we would have understood them. But the *feeling.* I understood that without any trouble.

A feeling of comradery. Of common purpose. A desire to bond and forge a friendship. I felt it not only from the alien who gestured, but from all of them inside the ship.

I also understood, either instinctively or because they were somehow telling us so, that they were not here to teach us like the aliens from the night before, but were simply here to meet us.

I could understand their curiosity. I was of course deeply curious about them. But I had no idea where to start, other than to keep staring at them while my own body phased in and out of view.

At last our leader, Dr. Proul, took command of the interaction.

"This is completely voluntary," he said, his voice dropping into the void with each word, "but they would like to scan you. It won't hurt you. It is their way of learning. I'll start, even though they've already scanned me many times."

Dr. Proul opened out his arms and held them away from his sides. I could see him standing there in blinks of white and yellow and green.

The alien who had greeted us with its gesture now stepped in front of Dr. Proul and lifted both its three-fingered hands to the height of Dr. Proul's face, and about six inches away from it.

The alien rounded its hands in a semi-circle that ended just past both of Dr. Proul's ears. And that was enough, apparently, because I could see a shimmering light begin to encase Dr. Proul's body from head to foot. As if he had stepped into a shower of pale white light that was now bathing his body even as it continued materializing and de-materializing as before.

The scan lasted only about a minute. When it was over, the pale white light melted away.

I don't know what got into me, other than my burning curiosity. I held up my hand like I was in school and said, "I'll do it."

A different alien, one that was closest to me, turned and took up its position in front of me and repeated everything I'd just seen.

I could feel it. Could feel the barest tingly touch of the light. It didn't hurt me. It felt neither warm nor cold. But in addition to the feeling of the light moving across my body, I thought I could feel some essence of me being pulled. Again, it didn't hurt. But it was noticeable. If this is what it felt like for information to flow from a human to another being, then I suppose I didn't mind.

Although I did wish I could perform the same kind of scan in reverse. I felt a little empty when it was over, because it felt so uneven.

But nothing gained if you don't try. Before the alien turned away to scan some other volunteer—and there were several now, after they watched it with both Dr. Proul and me—I copied the gesture I had watched twice now. I raised my palms above my head, level with the alien's face, and raised my eyebrows in some show of asking for permission.

The alien bent its head to the side. I took that to mean I could try. I circled my hands up and away around the alien's oblong head.

But I was human, not alien, and the magic didn't work for me. There was no corresponding shower of pale white light surrounding it, and I felt no information coming into my mind.

It was interesting that the alien let me try it that way first, because as soon as I failed, it did it the right way.

It pressed its first and longest finger against my still raised right index finger. Just a light and momentary touch. That was all it took.

I saw stars whiz by. Galaxies. Moons and planets and smaller chunks of space matter that might have been asteroids or other lone stars. Like a sped-up movie sequence meant to show an out-of-body experience or beyond-the-speed-of-light space travel. Too fast for me to take in any individual sight, but overall a concept of great distance and the incredible beauty of going from wherever they came from to here.

By now most of my fellow scientists were taking their turns being scanned. I saw Claudette watching with a look of nervous concern.

The interior of the ship was pleasantly warm, but all of us humans were overdressed. The aliens of light didn't need any clothes. But they also didn't appear to be sweating like I could now smell among us.

I wondered what the aliens thought about that. If it was like humans visiting a farm and either recoiling from or being charmed by the smells of horses and cows and chickens.

I locked eyes with Claudette and gave her an encouraging smile. She smiled back, wanly, and subtly shook her head. No scanning for Claudette, that was clear. But like Dr. Proul said, it was purely voluntary. No one was trying to force anyone to do anything.

I suppose there must have been a longer agenda for the night. First the greeting, then scanning, then some kind of mutual interaction. Maybe the other scientists would have done what I did, and ask to scan the aliens in return. Maybe the aliens would have taught us about where they came from. How their ship worked. How, if I was right, their ship was actually alive.

Dr. Proul must have projected some vision of how the night would go. He had done this before, I assumed, with these same aliens, and must have had some sense of the great progress humans could make just from spending a few hours in the presence of these gentle and presumably greatly-advanced creatures.

I could already imagine returning to the house after it was all over, and drinking down a full bottle of water, and discussing with all of my colleagues what they felt tonight and what they learned.

But none of that happened.

None of it went according to anyone's plan.

Because suddenly Sheila shouted into the deadening airspace, "THEY'RE HERE! EVERYBODY RUN!"

9

Nine scientists stood frozen and confused. Only Sheila and Dr. Proul leapt into immediate action.

They began pushing the other scientists toward the edges of the ship. There was no door. Most of us only just then realized it.

But the ship was a living, sentient being, and the aliens inside it meant us no harm.

Whether it was by their direction, or if the ship did it on its own, suddenly the walls faded into thin streaks of pale green light that we humans could run through, back out into the snowy night.

We didn't know why we were running. We only had Sheila's yelled warning to go by.

But as soon as we exited the sound-deadening ship, we found that our whole area was under attack.

There were two planes above us. Military jets, from the look of them. Small and black and angular, like arrows with wings. They were shooting at the ship, but not with any kind of armament I had ever heard of.

It struck the dome of the ship and the ground around it with the kind of deafening violence of a bolt of lightning. The ground shook beneath our feet. I fell into a crouch and covered my head with my arms. Other scientists heeded Sheila's words and started running in the snow. But then came another bolt of lightning, shot from one of the jets, and it lit up the snow and threw people off their feet.

I continued cowering in a huddled ball. Others around me were doing the same. I wondered what was happening back inside the ship, and I risked looking back the way we came.

It had compressed again into a glowing orange sphere. The size of a basketball. But still vulnerable as we all were.

The bolts of lightning continued raining down on our collective group. People were screaming and crying and begging the jets to stop.

Dr. Proul was suddenly crouched beside me. He shielded me with his arm against my back. "Stay here!" he shouted over the din of screaming and cracks of lightning. Then he ran on to the next crouching person to tell them the same.

And then I heard the crack of gunfire. Maybe rifles. I couldn't say. But lots of them, and coming from the ground.

I could see flashes coming from the darkness off to my left. Then another bolt of lightning from above. And more answering gunfire.

I was in a war zone suddenly, and nothing made sense. Not the jets above, not the gunfire from the ground.

Another bolt from the jets barely missed the glowing orange sphere. The lightning struck the ground so close to me I could smell the ozone.

I wasn't yelling or crying like any of the other scientists. I felt dazed and angry and afraid.

Then there were people rushing closer, and they brought the gunfire with them. I could see their shapes, dark against the snow, and see them aiming their rifles up toward the jets.

It was insane. None of it made sense. And then I saw Sheila scurrying among the people with rifles, aiming some kind of pistol into the air.

She shot at the closest jet. I could see a blue light flash from the barrel of her gun. But it had no impact. The jets seemed unaffected.

Why she had any kind of gun was confusing. Why she had something that wasn't a normal gun was only slightly more confusing.

The orange sphere was gone. I didn't see it leave. But apparently whoever was piloting the jets did. One of them took off, leaving the second one behind. Sheila shot at the remaining one with her strange gun, and this time it made contact.

There was a sizzling sound. Like a flame doused in water. The jet pulled up and flew a short distance away.

"Okay, go!" Dr. Proul shouted, and he was trying to direct traffic. Some of the scientists ran at a crouch, as if they expected someone to shoot at their heads.

They took off toward the house, which was still a long way away. But at least they were moving. They must have felt that was progress.

Our respite was short. The two jets both returned. Another bolt of lightning hit the ground, and then I saw why.

The orange sphere was gone, but there were still two silvery-white softball-sized spheres hovering above us, halfway between the ground and the attacking jets.

I wondered if they would remain small, or if they would expand back to the size of VW Bugs the way they did the night before.

Stay small, I wanted to tell them. Harder to hit. But more to the point, why were they there at all? Why didn't the smaller ships leave when the big one did?

I counted ten people on the ground wearing dark clothing and shooting rifles. Sheila had the only strange pistol. Why she was running around with the others, aiming at the jets, I had no idea. It was as shocking as all the rest of it.

And then finally the jets made contact. Or at least one of their bolts of lightning did. I saw it strike one of the scientists cowering in the snow.

The impact threw his body upward and I watched him land hard on his back. And then Jorge just lay there. He didn't get up.

"Somebody!" I shouted. "Look!" I pointed in the darkness as if that might help.

But Sheila had seen it, too. She rushed over to Jorge and covered him with her torso. I saw her feel for a pulse at the side of his neck.

Then she got up and ran on, back to the others with their rifles aiming at the jets. I stared at the outline of Jorge against the pale snow. He still wasn't moving. The shock of it was starting to sink in. Dr. Jorge Diaz was dead. Killed in front of my eyes.

Then. I saw one of the silvery-white spheres speed over to Jorge's body. And the next thing I saw was Jorge rising up into the air. His body was limp as a ragdoll. Something was pulling him from his center. His head and legs hung down lower as he continued rising through the dark.

But not for very long. The silvery-white sphere expanded briefly and just enough. It seemed to swallow Jorge whole. Then it shot off into the sky. Like an ambulance racing away. Or like an alien ship, claiming a human.

I scanned the sky for the other silvery-white sphere. It had to be around there somewhere. When one of the people in black fell to the next bolt of lightning from the jets, the silvery-white sphere sped right to it and repeated what I saw with Jorge. First the lifting of the body, so that it floated upward into space. Then the expansion of the sphere until it was large enough to absorb it.

Then the sphere shot off into the sky. What if another human fell? What if it was me? Would I hope the sphere would come take me, or not? I had no idea what was happening. It was all utter chaos.

Sheila must have gotten another hit with her strange pistol, because I could hear the sizzling sound again. One of the jets moved away, maybe to get out of range.

"Okay, move!" Sheila shouted, and Dr. Proul hustled the

rest of the remaining scientists away from the clearing. I ran in a crouch, too, even though I doubted it would help.

My breath was heaving in my chest. I could see little pricks of light popping in front of my eyes. My body was in full panic now, and who could blame it? I'd watched two people die in the last few minutes.

I could hear gunfire behind me. And another thunderous crash of lightning. I heard the fight continuing all the way on my run to the house.

Martin, one of my fellow physicists, was standing just inside the front door. He helped me up the steps and into the house.

A sob hitched inside my throat. Jorge was dead. I saw it happen.

I sank down stunned into my customary chair. Even in a crisis, we all cling to the familiar.

Then the house shook with an explosion somewhere back in the field. We all jerked around in that direction. I could see an enormous fire ball out the window and off in the distance. Maybe it was one of the jets. Maybe Sheila finally shot one down.

I looked around at my fellow scientists and saw their wide, panicked eyes. No one spoke. We all just breathed hard and tried to calm down.

Claudette covered her face with her hands and began to cry. Some of the men looked ashen and sick with fear. None of us were dealing with it well. My heart was still pumping far too hard.

Images started running through my brain. Of what I saw and heard. What I thought it all meant.

The truth was, I didn't have a clue. I didn't know who was in the jets or who was shooting at them from the ground.

I had no idea why Sheila suddenly shouted to us from inside the ship. How did she know we were in danger? I never heard anything at all.

The front door burst open again. Dr. Proul raced into the house. His hair was wet with sweat and snow. His dark sweater was torn, showing a strip of a white shirt underneath. His boots were caked with snow. He had a wild look on his face. The man who had serenely guided us through the past few extraordinary days now looked as lost and afraid as we did. It wasn't good to see.

"Listen!" he told us. "I know you've all had a shock, but I'm afraid it's not safe here anymore. I need you all to be ready to leave as soon as you can. Ten or fifteen minutes."

"But ... I can't drive these roads in the dark—" one of the men started to argue, but Dr. Proul cut him off.

"We have people to take you," he said. "They'll be here soon. I'm sorry I don't have time to discuss this. I need you to go get ready to leave. Now!"

"Hold on!" Martin the physicist shouted. "No! You wait! What's going on? Where are they taking us? What just happened out there?"

I could see that Dr. Proul had to forcibly bring himself under control. He still had his hand on the knob of the door, ready to yank it open and fly back into the night to deal with whatever he needed to deal with.

But the rest of us were on Martin's side. We needed to

know. Proul couldn't just leave us and make us figure it out. We deserved to know.

Dr. Proul's voice was tight with stress. I had to strain to hear what he said, he rattled it off so quickly. He seemed to resent having to give us even that extra minute.

"They've never gone this far before," he said. "They killed two people. The aliens will take care of them, but now everything has changed. And now we've killed people, too. It isn't safe here for you, do you understand? They know who you are. They'll come looking for you. Here, and back where you live.

"So you need to decide. Whether to go public in a big way, talk about all of this, hope that keeps you safe—or go into hiding. Maybe for the rest of your lives. I'm sorry, I truly am, I didn't want any of this to happen, but those are your only options. There's no middle ground anymore."

"Wait, what are you saying?" one of the other scientists shouted out. "Who's *they*?" But it was too late. Dr. Proul had already escaped.

For a moment the group of us sat in stunned silence. But then I bolted to my feet. Time was ticking away. My heart was beating out the time in rapid, panicked pulses, urging me to *go go go!* Nothing made sense, but I couldn't let that stop me.

"We'll figure it out later," I told everyone. "We need to get out of here. You heard that explosion, you heard the gunfire. He's right. It isn't safe. So do what you want, but I'm packing my bag."

Then I let my adrenaline speed me up the stairs. I wasn't made for running, but I can do it when I have to.

I heard footsteps behind me. Good. But it was up to them what they wanted to do. This was self-preservation. Not a damn faculty meeting.

When I got to the third floor I saw movement to my left, way down at the end of the hallway. The couple was back, by way of whatever secret entrance they took. The woman from Pepperdine and the aircraft designer from Seattle. And with them, helping the limping man get to his room, was Sheila.

I wanted to pretend I hadn't seen them. Some instinct told me not to get involved. I needed to get to my room and pack my bag and get out.

But Sheila hailed to me. "Angela! Wait." Then she hurried up the hallway. Against the urging of my nerves I stood in front of my door and waited.

As Sheila got closer I could see there was blood on her left cheek and above it, clumping together a patch of her ash-blonde hair.

"You're hurt," I said. "Come in. Let me get a washcloth on that."

But Sheila waved me away. "I'll take care of it in a minute. I need to talk to you. Hurry."

She ushered me into my room. I turned on the light and looked at her dirty, bloody face.

I remembered my initial impression of her the first day. The way she dressed and looked so impeccably groomed made her seem so corporate compared to a dowdy old professor like me.

But now I saw her with fresh eyes, a warrior come in from the field.

"Proul said we all have to leave now," I told her.

"You do. Go ahead and pack. I'm just going to sit for a minute."

She sank onto the edge of my bed. Her dark clothes looked wet with snow and mud and blood. The wound on her head had stopped bleeding, but her blonde hair still looked matted from what was already there.

Now that I knew to look for it, I could see the outline of her strange pistol in the pocket of her coat. She still wore her black leather gloves, and I had a flash of understanding. They were so impractically thin for the cold weather because she needed to be able to pull the trigger without them interfering.

I began shoving loose clothing into my roller bag. I still wore my boots from earlier. I was still wearing everything from before, including my teal ski coat. The whole outfit was making me hot inside the room, but I didn't dare take time to strip anything off. I would be leaving quickly. Which meant Sheila and I didn't have long to talk.

"I need you to know that Dr. Diaz is all right," she said.

"I saw him die!" I wasn't interested in being lied to. Placated. By anyone. I shoved my notebook into my laptop bag. "Then I … I saw him rising. I saw him taken up."

"I know," Sheila said. "They took one of my men, too. They'll both live—the ETs will heal them. But we won't see them again. They're gone."

I stopped packing and stared at her. "What are you saying? And what do you mean, one of your men?"

Then I got to the real point, the one that I think I already knew was the real issue. "Who are you?" Because it seemed fairly clear she wasn't just the senior scientist at a telecommunications company in Omaha, Nebraska.

I heard a door slam from somewhere down below. Maybe it was Dr. Proul returning to hustle us along.

I glanced around the room, anxious that I was leaving things behind. But I had traveled fairly lightly and I seemed to have regathered it all.

"We'll talk in the car," Sheila said. "I'm one of the drivers. But I prefer if it's just you and me. I wanted to catch you before you went with somebody else. Will you trust me? I'll try to explain as best as I can."

She seemed exhausted and sincere. But I wasn't sure what to do.

"People! We need to leave!" Dr. Proul shouted up from the first floor.

Sheila stood and went to the door. "Angela? Will you trust me?"

I waited for some internal instinct to tell me what to do.

Over my lifetime I have heard the still, small voice inside me often enough I have come to rely on it in times of crisis.

But I heard nothing, felt nothing, apparently I was on my own.

I had to decide. So I did. I nodded.

Sheila seemed relieved. She reached for my bag.

Then she opened my door and looked to the right and left, as if making sure the coast was clear.

"Come on," she whispered.

And so I followed.

Sheila walked quickly and quietly down the length of the hallway, past the stairs where I could see other scientists already hurrying down to the main floor.

When we reached the second-to-last room at the far end of the hall, Sheila knocked once on the door. The woman from Pepperdine opened it.

"How is he?" Sheila asked.

"Not mobile," the woman answered. She gave me a curt nod. I just stared back.

She claimed to be a physicist, but now I doubted that, too. If Sheila wasn't who she said she was, then who else had lied?

I could see the airplane designer from Seattle—if that's who he really was—lying with his eyes closed, covered up in bed.

"Stay with him," Sheila said. "I'll be in touch later."

The woman from Pepperdine nodded and closed the

door. Sheila continued on to a door that looked like the ones on all the other rooms, but when she opened it I could see a set of dark concrete stairs.

A light came on automatically.

"Careful," Sheila said. "Steps might be slick."

They were. From all the sets of boots that came in from the snow. But I held on to the banister and Sheila continued carrying my luggage down the three floors.

The door at the bottom opened out into the dark snowy night. I could hear car motors to the left, toward the front of the house.

Sheila started moving along the side of the house. Now that we were outside, she wasn't in much of a hurry.

When she was close enough she could look around the corner toward the parking area, she paused and held up her hand for me to wait.

I saw three large black SUVs pulling away from the house and driving out through the snow. There were faces at the windows in the back of the vehicles. There should have been seven scientists leaving, now that Jorge Diaz was gone and Sheila and I were hiding at the side of the house. Three large SUVs seemed more than they needed for just seven people, but maybe they were going to different destinations.

"We'll take my car," Sheila said. She led me to a dark-colored Toyota 4Runner parked last in the row of the various rentals.

She opened the back door on the driver's side and threw my roller bag on the seat. She got in and I sat in the front passenger seat.

Then we were rolling. I put on my seatbelt and twisted around to look back. I could still see the glow of whatever was burning out in the darkness.

"Was that one of the jets?" I asked.

"They weren't jets," Sheila said. "Jets can't hover like that. They were ARVs. Alien Reproduction Vehicles." She sighed. "There's a lot to tell you."

"Can I ask you something first?" I said. Sheila nodded. "Why me? Why are you taking just me, and not any of the others?"

"Because I need to have a private conversation. I've been asked to look for you. To make contact."

"Asked? By who?" I said. This whole situation was getting more bizarre by the moment.

"A friend of mine. Reggie Swan. We have a long drive. Let me try to fill in some of the pieces. First, my name isn't Sheila Rash. It's Kirsten Simmens. I work for the government. One of the agencies. I'm sorry I can't say which one."

I felt like I was suddenly in a movie. None of this seemed real.

Whereas everything that had come before—three nights of spaceships and aliens, then tonight's battle out in the snow—all of that felt absolutely real. It was just now, with the adrenaline wearing off, that my logical mind was trying to assert itself. But it was going to have to go along with all of this a while longer.

"Why were you here?" I asked Sheila—Kirsten, I would have to start thinking of her now. "What did you mean that the aliens took one of your men?"

Kirsten continued navigating the snowy mountain road

in the pitch dark and didn't answer me for several long moments.

Then she said, "A lot of this was my fault. I shouldn't have stayed inside the ship with all of you tonight. But … I got caught up in it. Those aliens were new to me. I just wanted to know."

"Of course you did." I understood at least that much. Anyone would have been mesmerized by what we saw.

"But I should have stayed outside with my team. I've been worried all day that something would happen. Just … not this bad. It's never been like this before."

"Dr. Proul said that, too."

"I've been to other conferences of his," Kirsten said. "This is my sixth one. I wasn't expecting that guy Bob Kennick to pull out a gun the first night. That already caught me off guard."

"Wait a minute," I said, remembering the two men in dark overcoats who had come to the door and hauled Bob the chemist away. "Were those your men who arrested him?"

"Not technically arrested," Kirsten said, "but yes."

"So where is he now?"

Kirsten gave a dismissive wave of her hand. "Safe. But I'm more interested in keeping Adam Proul safe. No time for nut jobs."

"So what's happened at the other conferences of his you've been to?"

"Military surveillance, for sure. Sometimes jets or helis buzzing the area. But never an attack like this." Kirsten rubbed her fingers over the dried blood in her hair. "This was another level."

"Why, do you think?" I asked.

Kirsten sighed. "I think they were jazzed to try out their new weapon."

"The lightning bolts?"

"EMDs. Electromagnetic Disrupters. They're supposed to interfere with extraterrestrial crafts. I think they could, if they actually hit them."

"But the ship changed back," I said. "It got smaller again."

"Right," Kirsten said. "Harder to hit. They can compress —you saw that—but they're also incredibly fast. So those idiots were just shooting at wherever they thought the ships were. Didn't matter that there were people down there."

"I saw you shoot back," I said.

"A smaller EMD. I hit them a few times."

"I saw. I heard it. A kind of sizzling. Was it you who shot down that jet?"

"Not a jet," Kirsten reminded me. "Alien Reproduction Vehicles are the military's attempt at copying alien craft. Did you actually see them?"

"I did." I thought of my impression of them as black arrows with wings.

"They've been trying for years to duplicate the speed and the maneuverability," Kirsten said. "They're not there yet, but they get closer all the time. That's why they come out to events like this. To try to shoot down another one and reverse engineer it."

"But there were aliens inside it," I said. "What happens to them?"

"Captured," Kirsten said. "Killed. Dissected." She turned to me in the dark car. "Why do you think I'm out here leading a team? I'm trying to keep it from happening."

I thought of the gentle creatures I had met over the past three nights. The green light from the first night touching my hand, filling me with whatever power helped me heal Dr. Proul after he was shot. The floating, glowing, radiant alien of the second night that reminded me of a sea angel. Then tonight's beams of light that formed into tall aliens who wanted to scan us, to satisfy their own curiosity.

I couldn't imagine any of them in the hands of soldiers or military medical personnel. I was beginning to understand the need for people like Kirsten and the woman from Pepperdine and the man from Seattle.

"How many people were on your team?" I asked.

"Ten," she said. "Not enough, now in retrospect." She gripped the steering wheel. "We're going to have to reassess after all this. If the threat is escalating, we have to, too."

It was a lot. A lot to take in. I could feel a heavy exhaustion seeping into my bones. My mind was starting to feel mushy. I needed to stop talking and let it all sink in.

I glanced at the clock on the dashboard. It was only a little after eleven. I was surprised it wasn't much later. So much had happened in such a short time.

"I need to rest," I said.

"Take your time," Kirsten answered. "We have a long ways to go."

I closed my eyes and leaned back against the seat rest. Images from the night started racing through my mind. I could feel pieces trying to form themselves into one coherent whole. But I didn't have nearly enough information. I was struggling with just bits of knowledge, and all of it was brand new.

I tried to relax and just let the miles disappear behind us into the darkness. I was glad not to be driving. Kirsten must have been exhausted, too.

In time I was ready for my answers. "So who are you?" I asked. "What is your job?"

"Technically? Field agent and team supervisor. Specifically? I coordinate with alien communication." She glanced toward me. Paused. "I can hear them. I understand them."

"Aliens."

"Yes. I could hear their ship tonight, too. It's what alerted me to the oncoming attack. It could hear it. Sense it."

I remembered thinking that the ship was sentient. So I wasn't surprised to hear it confirmed.

But I still couldn't quite grasp what Kirsten was telling me. "You can communicate with aliens?"

"It's … an ability I have," Kirsten said. "The Agency has made good use of it. I go where people are making contact. Like Adam Proul. He's always successful at it. I'm there to make sure the interaction goes well. I'm there to protect the ETs, if you want to know the truth."

"Protect from who?" I said. "Dr. Proul?"

"Not at all. He's a friend to extraterrestrials, just like I am. Just like you are, I assume."

"I am," I said emphatically. "Of course." Although if anyone had asked me where I stood on that just a few days ago, I would have treated it like a hypothetical, like so many notions in science. Do you believe in time travel? In multiverses? Oh sure, I believe they're *possible*...

"So who are you protecting them from?" I asked. "Who were those guys tonight?"

"They were ours, technically," Kirsten said. "Our military. Our government. There are certain forces—people in power—who don't want peaceful communication. They want war. They want reasons to build more weapons and use them here and out in space. I know this sounds crazy—"

"It doesn't," I said. "I just feel completely ignorant about the world. I live in a bubble. I've just been doing my science all these years. Go on. Tell me."

Kirsten sighed. "There's a lot to this, but let me just talk about tonight. Their goal is always to shoot down more spacecraft and capture more aliens and kill them. It's a passion with more people than you imagine. Domination. Another kill. They get high on it. But the official line is that they're protecting us—from what? You saw who these aliens are. Do they seem like a threat to you?"

"No," I said. "Not at all."

"I'm not saying all of them are fuzzy bunnies and puppies," Kirsten said. "Just like we have our share of predators on Earth. Sharks, snakes—other planetary systems have them, too. But for the most part, the ETs coming here to make contact are doing it to try to help their younger brothers and sisters along. Us. We're a younger, more primitive version of what they are. I've talked to them. I know."

"We're ... them? They're future us?" I had never heard anything like that. It was such a radical idea, I felt a little queasy at the thought.

Not because I didn't want it. I'm all for human evolution. The faster the better—get us away from all this war and violence and brutality. If there's a better, peaceful future waiting for us, I'm all for taking the quickest route there.

But Kirsten was right, it did sound crazy, the more she kept talking. I could imagine some of my colleagues from this weekend's conference balking at it, even after everything we all saw.

"I'm telling you all this—I'm telling you the truth," Kirsten said, "because of what you told me about your father's healing."

I had made good on my promise to share the details of that with her earlier in the day. The fact that she listened with rapt interest kept me going, even though I rarely tell other scientists about it. I've learned over the years to be careful. But she hadn't scoffed at me or rolled her eyes or done any of the things I'd seen other scientists do. So yes, I'd told her everything. And now, apparently, this was my reward.

"I know you're open minded," Kirsten said. "I'm not surprised. Reggie Swan told me you would be."

"Who the hell is Reggie Swan?" I blurted out. I'd forgotten all about that piece of the puzzle. "I've never heard of him. Why would he tell you to come looking for me?"

Kirsten surprised me by chuckling. It was a welcome, and stress-reducing, sound.

"Oh, Angela, we are really going down the rabbit hole now," Kirsten said. "Are you sure you're ready for it?"

"Might as well," I said. "Pile it on."

"He's a ship designer. Aircraft ship. Okay, I'll just say it. Spaceship."

"Spaceship," I repeated. So far I was still following.

"This is where it gets a little squirrely," Kirsten said. "He's been using your design for Pure Dark Energy to power his spaceships. For about ten years now. Ten years ... *from* now, but also *before* now. It's ... a little hard to explain."

I sighed. "Not really. I'm a theoretical physicist. I've read other people's papers. I've played around with all sorts of mind experiments. You're talking about a time loop, I assume."

"Yes!" Kirsten said, sounding relieved that I already got it. "That's exactly what Reggie said it is."

"It's a chicken and egg problem," I said. "Advanced technology from the future, brought back to the past, to create the technology in the future."

I had a physicist friend out in Oakland, California who was absolutely obsessed with the whole idea. We had talked about it over food and coffee many, many times. Kirsten wasn't broaching something brand new. Aliens, yes, those were new. But time loops, try me on something I don't know.

"So now we come to a decision point," Kirsten said. I could hear the engine of the 4Runner revving as it dragged us up a steep stretch of the road. I hadn't been paying much attention to where we were. Everything still looked dark and remote as the road curved and carved through the snowy mountains.

"Reggie would like to meet you," Kirsten said. "He's waiting at a place near Salt Lake City. I'm prepared to drive you there. I don't think it's safe for you to fly anywhere now. Your name might be flagged."

"It's that serious?" I asked. I could feel anxiety welling up in my gut again.

"Yeah," Kirsten said. "Afraid it is."

"What did Dr. Proul mean," I asked. "About all of us having to either go into hiding or going public in a big way? I-I have a life. Back in Madison. I'm not interested in leaving it."

"I know," Kirsten said. "But tonight changed things for all of us. People were killed. You saw that. Or at least, temporarily dead. I promise you, Jorge Diaz is alive again by now. So is my field agent, Roger. But questions are going to be asked. What happened to Dr. Diaz? You've seen too much tonight. All of you have."

"And that makes us dangerous to someone?"

"Very," Kirsten said. "You have no idea who all these players are. But it is well within their capacity to show up at your house or office and make sure it looks like you had a heart attack. I'm sorry. I wish it wasn't so. But it is."

It's not the kind of thing you want to hear. It's frightening, of course—it would be to anyone. But it's also being informed of a different kind of death. The death of your whole life and everything you've made it to be over the years. I have a nice place to live. A good position on the faculty at UW-M. I have friends. Distant family. I don't want to disappear. I don't want my life to disappear from me.

But Kirsten Simmens wasn't some kook telling me a fantasy story. She was the real thing. This whole thing was real.

I could feel a wave of sadness and fear welling up inside me, ready to engulf me. Too soon. Too fast. It was all happening too fast. I have a sharp mind, but this was too much for it all at once.

Kirsten glanced aside at me. "I understand," she said quietly. "I really do." She reached over and squeezed my left hand. "I'm sorry, Angela. This isn't how it should be."

My voice came out strangled. "But it is. That's what you're saying. It just is."

"Yes. I can't pretend. You're in danger, and I want to protect you. Reggie Swan will help protect you."

I turned to her in the dark car. "How? How can he protect me?"

"It's a place to hide," Kirsten said. "Where he is. You can stay there."

"For the rest of my life?" The impact was hitting me full on now. I felt like someone who had just been told they had two weeks to live. I needed more time. I needed to say goodbye. I needed, I needed…

"It's a time loop," Kirsten reminded me. "So…"

A time loop. Right. If she was right. They weren't proven, of course, they were just theoretical.

But so was Pure Dark Energy at one time, just a line in some schlocky science fiction movie. And I had made that real. Just by envisioning it and then working to bring it into being. You have to have a certain kind of mind. One that is willing to stretch and twist and roll around back on itself.

I have that kind of mind. I always have. Maybe this was why. This very moment. Maybe this was exactly why I was made the way I was.

Open to the miraculous. Open to the inexplicable. Open to what I had experienced over the past three nights. Open to wonder and to knowledge of things I couldn't have imagined before.

Like Dr. Adam Proul asked us on our first evening together. Why are we alive now? Why are we here in these times?

Because I can take it. Because I'm not afraid to believe what I see. Because I'm not afraid to know what I know.

"So you're saying I might not be stuck in this time." Maybe I didn't have to leave my old life forever. But it was a risk. As are all theoretical constructs. You believe them at your mental and professional peril.

"I don't know," Kirsten said. "You'll have to talk to Reggie about that. He has a lot to say about it. He has some … experience."

We drove through the night. I slept for a while, even though I felt too keyed up to let go for long. We stopped once for gas and to fuel ourselves with giant cups of coffee.

I took my turn at the wheel so Kirsten could rest. Then she took over again.

It was still dark in the early hours of the morning when we crossed the border into Utah. At an abandoned gas station outside a small town whose sign I didn't even notice, there was a white Ford Explorer, maybe a few years old, waiting with the key duct taped under the back fender. Kirsten transferred my roller bag from the 4Runner to the Explorer and we continued our drive.

"You think someone was following us?" I asked.

"Protocol," Kirsten said. "Don't worry about it."

We stopped for more gas and coffee and food in Moab. I drove for a while and let Kirsten sleep.

The terrain was dry and very different from my wintery Madison life. Lots of red rock and dramatic rock formations. I felt like I was driving on another planet.

As the wheels beat out a rhythm against the black top, I could feel my mind coming back online. It had had time to sort through all the new data, it seems, and was ready to discuss with me what it found.

I was on my way to meet someone who was using my theory of Pure Dark Energy to fuel his spacecrafts. He was making things. Not just theorizing. Which meant that someone else—even if it was just one person in the whole world—knew that what I had created actually worked.

Which meant I had taken a step forward, without even knowing it. Forward toward the future I had been imagining for the past forty years.

Or as Dr. Proul put it, projecting myself into a future where anyone in the world, poor or rich, educated or not, technically savvy or not, could harness free, pure energy and improve their lives. Move the human race forward.

Why was I alive right now? Maybe to meet Reggie Swan, whoever he was. Maybe to meet Adam Proul and Kirsten Simmens. Maybe to have my entire life upended, just like it is now, and have to start at a new place. But not start over. I wasn't back to square one. I was bringing all my knowledge and experience with me.

Now that the shock was over, I could feel my excitement build.

It was exactly what my father did for us, back when I was thirteen. He realized we couldn't remain in our little town anymore, now that he had been miraculously cured. The people there wouldn't accept it, they couldn't believe it, and rather than fight their narrow, stubborn minds, it was better to just pull up stakes and leave.

I have been fighting with my scientific peers for years now, trying to get them to see that what I've discovered is real. What I've made from it is real.

But maybe that was always a losing fight. Maybe the best course was always to pull up stakes and go find the people who would listen to me and believe.

It felt right to watch the sun rise over the alien-looking rocks.

I drove on. Toward the future. Toward my future. And toward the future I can imagine for us all.

SECOND LIFE

1

Your hair is a snarled mass of gray. Your clothes are rumpled. You've barely slept. You look exhausted.

"Not at my best," you warned me. "I'll look so dowdy. Even older than I am." But all I see is a beautiful woman standing before me. The lines and creases on your face are precious to me. Your eyes take me in with that curiosity you bring to everything in your life: Who is this man? Why does he want to meet me?

And what is this place?

We stand in the hangar of the Factory, four of us: You and me and my friends Kirsten Simmens and Fritz Zimholt, who owns this facility.

You're unsure. You're still bundled up against the cold. Outside, the Wasatch mountains of Utah are covered in a record depth of snow. Inside, underground, we're warm and protected. But all of this is new to you. So you still wear your green ski coat. But you took off your gloves.

You're not wearing a ring. I knew you wouldn't, but your finger looks so bare without it. It catches my eye.

There are people moving about, tending to their work on the various aircraft down here, pilots and mechanics and at least fifty personnel, and you take it all in with your curious gaze.

Then you turn your eyes back to me.

You don't remember me. There's no reason you should. We hatched this meeting years ago. This date, this place, this aftermath of what you just experienced in the mountains of Colorado.

But I have been busy all this time, seeding myself along your path over the last few years. I came to several of your conferences. We never spoke. But I was the tall black man out in the crowd nodding as you explained your theories. I wasn't like your colleagues, scowling at your brilliant ideas.

I was the man in the grocery store in Madison, Wisconsin a few times, reaching for something off a high shelf for you that you couldn't quite reach yourself.

That self-conscious laugh. "Thanks." Always that genuine smile. How I loved you.

So many times we could have met along this time line, but I had to hold back. We always knew it had to be right. It had to be like this, in this exact moment, or nothing would work the way we wanted it to.

I told you in the beginning, the first time we met, what my strategy was. "I'm going to be nice to you."

That took you by surprise. As if no one had ever tried that before. But you settled right into it. You softened and leaned back. You let me love you sooner than you might otherwise. I'm a maker by nature, and this was a love worth making.

Not just once, but again. As many times as I'm allowed.

We talked about your theory that every choice exists, and every choice is made. Which means there are timelines when we never meet. Others where we meet and don't connect.

Unacceptable, sweetheart, as I've told you.

So even though this was meant to be a clean choice, completely unweighted on either side, I'll admit I have done a few things to skew it.

Not so much that I worry I've ruined your chance at a fresh loop of time, but enough to maybe help us along.

So I have been that face in the crowd, that approving nod, that friendly stranger who helped you for a moment and moved on. I figured it would create echoes. A subtle familiarity so that today, in this moment, you would look at me the way you are, wondering if you know me.

"Dr. Corliss," I say, extending my hand. "Reggie Swan. So good to meet you."

"Angela, please." That smile I know so well, even though you look worn to the bone. It's been a hard, hard night for you.

You knew it would be. You already did it once in your other life. But you said you had to do it again. Do it right. Last time you left early. Last time, you told me, you were a coward. This time you were going to stay and learn all of it.

We shake hands. This hand of yours that I've held tenderly thousands of times. The knuckles I have raised to my lips to kiss. "Courtly," you told me once. That's right, ma'am. You deserve every formal demonstration of love.

How did I find you the first time? My friend RayJay showed me the key. Searching with my heart across time and space, not knowing who I was supposed to be looking for, but just letting my time map—my heart map—lock onto you.

Heart, mind, body and soul. Everything I could ever want from a love.

And clearly my intellectual superior, even though you still refuse to admit it. I might be able to make nearly anything I set my hand to, but I needed your mind to help me figure out the missing parts.

Your Pure Dark Energy. I couldn't have made any of this without you. Nothing in this hangar. All of these experimental aircraft, the spacecraft, are here because of you.

There are so many more things I need to make, and I need you still. Again. But over here in a second time loop. It's your theory, not mine: how to take the gains of the past several years and add to them now with new knowledge, new ideas. And that way go further.

You had a strange way of explaining it. Like a person dying and coming back into their already existing body. Reincarnating in place.

"That way you don't have to waste time being a baby and a teenager and going through all that again," you said. "You bank the gains. But you start over and let it take you further. Higher."

"Why can't we just go on the way we are?" I asked you.

Stopping, starting over—it made no sense. And I resisted having to lose you, even temporarily.

"Because we both already took certain paths," you said. "We already used up a bunch of years. I need a fresh loop. Start someplace different. You have to trust me on this."

The old you made herself an expert on time loops. This new you is still skeptical about them. You told me that was the way.

"We all get too entrenched in our ways of habitual thinking," you said. "The only way forward is to break free."

Reincarnate in place. Stop, begin again, find each other again.

And so here we are, at last. I tell you a little about this place, the Factory. I talk to you as if I don't know you. As if you haven't been my wife for ten years. I want to kiss you. Hold you. The others don't know, Fritz and Kirsten. Not in this timeline. Think how shocked they would be if I just reached for you now and brought us both back where we belong.

You yawn. You can't help it. You cover your mouth and look embarrassed.

"You must be bushed," I say. "And here I am talking."

"I just need a short rest," you say. "But then I want to hear everything. Of course. I need to know all of this."

I offer to show you to your room. It's down two floors, deeper underground, down where Fritz keeps the guest quarters for people like me passing through.

But I'm not just passing through this time. I'll be staying a good long while. You couldn't tear me away.

I wish I could hold your hand as we descend the stairs. I wish I could put my arm around you and pull you in close against my hip, the way we liked to be. We fit perfectly together. We always have.

"Oh, I do remember," you say suddenly as we round the corner and head toward your room.

You stop in the hallway and look up at me. I don't know what to say. What to do. This wasn't how we planned.

"You told me you're an Orioles fan," you say. And I let out a surprised laugh.

"I never said that."

You squint your beautiful, intelligent eyes at me and give me that smile I'm never tired of.

"Then something," you say. "I remember you from somewhere." You yawn again. "I'll think of it. I just need to sleep."

I leave you at your room. I show you how to make an imprint of your hand on the panel inset in the door. "It'll open just for you." *And anyone else you want to let in.* I think it but don't say it. But I would give a million dollars to come in with you right now.

We've been separated too long. You said it had to be that way so your mind would let you forget.

I give you a little bow. "Good night, then."

You smile. I almost expect you to say *How courtly,* but you don't.

I have to leave you and take my aching heart back up the stairs.

2

I fell asleep so hard and so fast, you would think someone beaned me over the head.

The room they gave me is sparse, easy on the eyes and nerves. I liked the country cabin effect of Dr. Adam Proul's mountain mansion, but right now seeing anything made of pine or oak wouldn't soothe me in the least. The white and gray room, the concrete walls, the sleek tile in the bathroom—everything looks modern and clean. A fresh start.

I fell asleep in my clothes. No idea how long I was out. I start the coffeepot on the bedside table and undress to go take a shower. The hot water feels like medicine. I wash my skin, my hair. I let the events of the past few days glide down the drain. That was then. This is now. All of that is over.

This place could be my place. All the activity, the technology, the *ideas*—as exhausted as I was when I first arrived, I felt a thrill through my veins. An energy I haven't found other places—even at Dr. Proul's conference. That was a different feeling all together. This—this feels like a plausible future for me.

There's something wickedly invigorating about being around sharp, elevated minds. The kind of people who not only accept the science I've been doing, but who *want* it. Want more of it.

And what of Reggie Swan? The man who asked Kirsten a.k.a. Sheila to look for me and pluck me out of that equally elevated crowd.

You have a feeling about people. The way I think animals know. This one hits … this one loves … this one will feed me and take me in. I saw it with my neighbor once, how a feral kitten came up to him and rubbed against his leg, no doubt ready to bolt at the first sign it had misjudged the man's character.

But the kitten was right to trust him. Peter and his wife took her in, bathed her, fed her, loved her for five perfect days, and then the kitten slipped away in the night, hid inside their bathroom vanity, and died there as she must have known she was about to do.

The vet said she wasn't a kitten at all, she was probably two years old already, based on her teeth, but she was so undernourished she never grew. On top of that, her little body was riddled with parasites. She was so sick and emaciated, she must have been right on the verge of starving that day she ran to Peter for help. Five perfect days. Probably the only days of her life that she felt safe and loved.

You get a sense about people. Kind, unkind. Nourishing or draining. Worth your time, not.

The people here seem good. I already felt fine about Kirsten Simmens, even though she lied to me. I get that it was necessary. Doesn't change who she is, deep down. At a conference I once heard a psychotherapist describe people's habitual behaviors as *characterological*. We are who we are. The liar lies. In their minds, it works. They will rarely feel motivated to change into someone honest. Honesty is for suckers.

But sometimes even honest people have to take another course. Some circumstance makes it feel like the only sensible option. Like that party game of asking people if it's ever all right to lie. For some people, it's black and white: *No, never.*

"So if there's a maniac in your house who wants to harm some member of your family, and that person—your father or mother or child—is hiding in a closet, and the maniac demands to know where your loved one is—do you have to tell the truth?"

Silence. Not so clear after all.

Sometimes good people, honest people, lie. But usually the behavior is brief. They can't sustain it. We are who we are.

Fritz Zimholt? I feel fine about him. He has a calm way about him. Steady at the helm. He's obviously ambitious enough to create this whole facility and staff it with so many talented people, but I've met my share of visionaries over the years who thought they were so brilliant they had the right to climb over anybody and anything on their way to the top. There's a kind of sickness that was always there. *Characterological.* Some people get power and they can't wait to use it to hurt people. To dominate.

Fritz Zimholt doesn't strike me as that kind at all. If he did, I'd already be gone, even if I knew he had unlocked all the secrets to the universe. Not everybody agrees with me, but knowledge isn't worth your soul. You still have to live with yourself. You have to know your limits.

And that takes me back to Reggie Swan.

I can see a starving kitty running up to that man. He just exudes safety and kindness. And to be both intelligent and competent on top of it—I'll admit when he was walking me down to my room last night my eyes strayed more than once to that wedding ring on his finger. Some woman is awfully lucky.

Which isn't normally the way I think. It's been *years* since I thought that way. The last time was probably in my thirties. No doubt some kind of hormonal prompting at the time from a body reminding me that if I wanted to have children, I'd better get after it. But the feeling passed, the colleague moved away, and I have never lacked a moment's worth of something to fill my time.

I know plenty of scientists, men and women, who have had to make the choice. Work suffers when there's a family wanting your attention. We all know it. But the lure is there. The temptation.

If you're lucky, like me, you don't have a real opportunity to choose. Makes it easy.

And then you get old. You make your discoveries. You

find satisfaction—deep satisfaction—in what your mind can actually accomplish.

And maybe some day you find out some stranger has actually used your ideas to make incredible things. And he wants to show you. And suddenly you find yourself in a strange place among strangers, feeling like this is exactly where you want to be. Where you would have chosen to be if you could have mapped it out yourself.

I've always had a hard time, scientifically, making up my mind about coincidence.

But there's still a thread of faith inside me, thin and deeply buried though it sometimes feels. The faith of a girl who saw her father healed by a preacher. The faith of a grown woman who had alien power flowing through her hands just a few nights ago that allowed her to bring a man back to life.

We don't know everything. None of us. Maybe we're not supposed to.

3

I'm in the hangar, talking to one of the mechanics, when I finally catch sight of you again. You've come up to find me, I think. I hope. Here I've been, waiting to be found.

You're in a worn pair of jeans and a rose-colored sweater. Your wavy gray hair looks damp from a shower. You look fantastic. It wouldn't be proper for me to say so.

"Afternoon," I say.

You laugh. "Is it?" You brush a strand of hair away from your left eye.

You polish up nicely. I've seen it so many times before. All you need is a good night's sleep, some good food, some good conversation—something invigorating to activate your busy mind—and your whole being seems to plump right up like a raisin reverting to a grape.

You used to be able to go for a whole week on very little sleep, but then it always caught up with you.

I'd notice the way your lids sloped so heavily over your eyes, the blinks coming slower and slower, and I'd cut off whatever we were talking about right in an instant and escort you to our bed.

Sometimes, especially if we were right in the middle of the juiciest of *What-if* science conversations, you'd protest mightily. But there was no arguing with me when it came to taking care of my wife.

"You'll thank me tomorrow," I'd say, knowing you probably wouldn't—you hated to suspend any fascinating talk—but I couldn't have your exhaustion on my conscience. You always knew I had your best interest at heart.

But you seem lively enough now. Restored. And I know, true to form, you're full of all sorts of questions.

Also true to form, you ask the hardest one first.

"Tell me about this time loop," you say, and when you notice even the smallest hesitation, you add, "Kirsten already mentioned it." As if to say, *Don't even think about trying to get out of this.*

But that isn't my hesitation. Lord knows I've thought how to tell you in multiple ways, long and short, intricate and simple. It's just that as of this moment, I still don't know which is best. It feels too important to just toss off any care and say whatever comes out of my mouth first.

So I stall a bit. "Let me show you first what we've made, thanks to you."

If we were both younger, you might roll your eyes. Instead you give me a withering look, but you do go along with it. Because I know you're curious about *everything.*

And what's in this hangar must be at least in the top five of that list.

I show you the current generation of pods. Not all of them are here right now. Some—a good dozen—are out in the cold mountain wind being put through their paces by the various test pilots. But there are still hundreds of pods sitting in neat rows on the clean concrete floor, lined up like so many beads on a string.

The top halves of the pods are transparent, allowing the pilots maximum visibility in all directions. The bottom halves are a dull opaque gray. The insides are a soft rose-gold color. Very soothing on the eyes.

The pods are made of a material not found here on Earth. Not in its raw state. I had to learn to duplicate it from the sample spacecraft flown here by my friends RayJay, Mit, and Linus. They came here for a just a few short years to share some of their technology with a few humans, like me.

It's an honor I treasure with all of my heart. One that you treasured too, once I brought you in on the project.

"I feel as if I know them," you told me more than once, back then. "I wish I could have met them."

You did meet them. Or at least they met you. You just didn't remember. You weren't supposed to.

Now, in this life, here you are stepping up to one of the pods for the very first time, examining it.

"These are all single-seaters," I tell you. "We have a few doubles, and we're working on some team transports that will hold four or five pods at a time."

You run your hand over the top of the nearest pod. I

know what it feels like: warm. Skin warmth. People notice that.

You pull your hand back for a moment, as if you don't quite believe it, then press your palm against the sphere again, harder.

"This isn't normal metal," you say.

"No." I wait. You like to figure things out for yourself.

"It almost feels…" You look up at me. Wanting to see my answer with your eyes. "…alive."

"It is," I say.

"Not a machine," you say.

"No. Not the way we think of one."

"A living entity."

I nod.

You blow out a soft breath. You turn back to the pod and crouch down to run your hand along the exterior. You peer inside the transparent domed lid to the soft golden-rose interior.

"Remarkable," you whisper. "Reggie."

When you turn back to me, your eyes are sparkling with wonder. Maybe even a little wet, the way they'd sometimes get when your mind took in some expansive truth.

Then you slowly stand back up, facing me. You cross your arms over your chest and tuck your hands underneath your armpits. I wonder if you're cold. The hangar isn't freezing, but it isn't exactly balmy. Normally I would warm your hands between my own. Instead I stand this close to you, pretending it doesn't matter. Pretending to be casual as I wait for your inevitable questions. I wonder which ones you'll ask first.

"Kirsten said you've been using my Pure Dark Energy for ten years."

"I have."

You shake your head and give a half-hearted smile. "I wish I'd known. I feel like I've been out in the wilderness all this time. I didn't know anyone even cared."

"It's complicated," I say. "Believe me, I would have loved to tell you."

I did tell you. I did love you. These pods brought us together.

"Tell me about the time loop."

"Also complicated," I say. "As you might imagine."

You let out another breath. Like you're steeling yourself to hear it. Like you're gathering your brain power to absorb it.

But I vowed I wouldn't tell you too much. You wanted this chance to be clean.

"I got as far as I could on my own," I tell you. I hate to lie to you, but the truth is too sticky. Not clean at all. You made me promise.

"Ten years ago, Kirsten said. And also … ten years from now?" You look up at me with your beautiful green eyes, ready to hear the full, amazing story.

"There abouts," I agree, looking over your left shoulder, as if something happening behind you has caught my attention. But it's just so I don't have to meet your gaze. You have a way of seeing right through me to the core. I couldn't even lie to you when the lie was for something sweet, like pretending I'd forgotten our anniversary so I could surprise you with a fancy dinner.

"I've been … in the wilderness too," I say. "On another planet, if you want to know the truth."

I let that sit. I'm hoping it will be enough of a distraction. But you're quiet for only a few moments, taking it in.

Then, "How did you get there?" I can see the hope written on your face. "With … my Pure Dark Energy?"

I shake my head no. I can see you're disappointed. "Ang—" I catch myself before calling you *Angie*. That's another life, not this one. Here I was expecting to call you Dr. Corliss for a while longer. "—gela," I continue, "I feel like it's going to take me hours to tell you the whole thing." *Hours and too many lies.* "But the short version: I met some extraterrestrials about ten years back. They brought some of their tech and taught me how to use it. Even … how to make it. But then they left, and it's taken me this long to find them on their own planet."

"But you did," you say, your voice quiet and low, the way it gets when you're excited but careful not to show it. The way you had to learn to be around your fellow scientists.

It makes me sad to see you do it to me. We shared everything. Neither of us ever held back.

"I did," I agree. "And they taught me even more—a lot more. Including how to skip back a year—" *Lie.* More than a year. "—and bring you in on this. If—that is, if you're willing to work with me."

And there's that smile again. It splits my heart in two. But it also lights me up like a bonfire. It's taking me everything I have not to reach out for you, fold you into my arms, hold you like I've been aching to do all this time we've been apart.

You stick out your hand. I was right, it's cold as I shake it.

"Reggie Swan," you say, "I'm happy to join the team. But now you're going to have to tell me absolutely everything."

Absolutely everything. Not even close. But I can tell you what you told me to say, and that will have to do.

First I stall some more. I'm not ready to rush into it.

"Do you want me to show you how these work?"

It's irresistible. I knew it would be. You allow me to distract you a little longer.

"What do you notice?" I ask, indicating the pod's soft rose-gold interior.

It only takes you a few seconds. "No controls?"

I shake my head and point at my temple. You smile. I knew you'd like it.

"Telepathy?"

"Yes," I say. "Good enough description."

"How? Can I think to it right now?"

"We have to pair you with one first," I say. "It needs to feel you inside it. Want to try one?"

You laugh. "Do you need to ask?"

"I'll open it," I say, showing off a little. I'm paired with all of the pods at the Factory, so any of them will respond to my thoughts.

Mentally, I ask the nearest one to open its lid. Not a command, but a request. *Please open. Thank you.*

More of my courtly manners, I suppose, but some of

the pilots had to learn the hard way that these craft can think for themselves. And they do not like being disrespected.

The lid smoothly glides open and tucks itself into the lower half. You reach out and touch the open rim. Always wanting to experience things for yourself.

I offer my hand to help you in. You take it.

Goddamn, woman, can't you feel it?

The way our fingers find each other so naturally. The energy that passes between our skin. The heat. The vibrancy. The *familiarity*.

I'm like a school boy having to hold back a racing heart and my panting breath. I hold onto your hand as long as seems decent, but then I let go before I say something I shouldn't.

You act like nothing's happened on your end. And maybe it's no act. Why should you feel a single thing for me? You only just met me yesterday, and that was while you could barely keep awake. If my little markers, showing up in your life here and there, have done anything to make you remember me, you sure don't seem affected.

I feel an unexpected deflation. What did I expect? Something. Not nothing.

You settle yourself into the seat of the pod.

I'm back to being your host.

"Rest your arms there," I say, pointing to the two projections at either side of the seat. "Let your hands extend over the edge of the arm rests. Try to let it get as much contact as it can with you ... that's right."

You shift a little, getting more comfortable. The arm

rests fold around your arms, gently cupping them from elbows to wrists. You give a little gasp of surprise. But then you smile. I know you. Of course you're delighted. A new toy. One that works in unexpected ways.

"Now your feet," I say. Before I can suggest it, you kick off your shoes. You don't go the extra step of removing your socks, but this is good enough. You rest your feet against the angled panel at the base of the pod.

"It's reading you," I tell you. "Just a little bit longer."

"This is the most comfortable chair I've ever sat in," you say.

"It would be. It always is for whoever's sitting there."

I give it a few minutes. Longer than it actually takes. But I want to give myself that same time. I need to keep a clear head. You don't know me. I have to remember myself.

"That should probably do it," I say.

"So what's next?"

"I find they like to be complimented."

You chuckle at that and look at me to make sure I'm not joking. I'm not.

"That's easy," you say. "Lots to admire."

You close your eyes for a bit. There's a soft smile resting on your lips.

Then you open your eyes again. "It's a she," you tell me.

"That she is," I say. "We have all kinds. Now see if she'll close her lid for you."

Your smile leaves. You're concentrating. It doesn't take a lot of effort. Just a simple straight-forward thought, and the lid of your pod glides up and over your head.

A second later, it glides back open. You must have asked it to.

"We used to use head gear," I say. "Fancy headbands to connect us to the pods. We thought we had to, to communicate with them. Turns out we were making it much harder than we had to."

"Don't I know that experience," you say. You hold your arm out to me, a signal you'd like help climbing back out of the pod. I clasp your hand again. My palm is sweaty. I'm sure you must be able to feel it. Damn school boy. If you knew me, we could laugh about it right now.

But if you notice, you're not letting on. Instead, you're right back to your original question. Dog with a bone, not giving it up.

As soon as I help you back on your feet and you're standing beside me: "The time loop," you say. "Tell me. We can get back to the pods later."

I suppress a sigh. In your place, I'd be the same. I'd want to know. No more fiddling around.

"Time loop is ten years," I say.

You watch my face, clearly expecting more. When I don't offer it, you narrow your eyes just a bit. Impatient.

"Kirsten said something about ten years ago *and* ten years from now."

I need to talk to that woman about not giving away all my punchlines.

"That's right," I tell you. "Twenty years so far, backward and forward."

"I don't pretend to know how that works," you say. "I

understand it, theoretically, but I've never been in a situation where someone can tell me it's real."

You look at me again, maybe willing me to say it still is a theory, we're not really sure, we *think* it might work this way…

But that would be a lie. "It's real," I say. "As real as you standing here."

Your eyes widen. But not out of fear or nervousness. I can see that. I know you're excited. Ready to learn something new, something big.

If you only knew the full truth. But I can't tell you all of it. You made me swear. I would never break my promise to you.

Even though I've been regretting it for the past several hours.

"Buy you a coffee?" I ask. Stalling. Still stalling.

But the offer lights you up. I know your head is probably pounding right now. Your caffeine addiction is real. Or at least was, in our other life. I wonder now if it still is. If maybe the many things I think I know about your aren't necessarily true this time.

I'm not sure I like that idea. But at the same time, it's also intriguing. Who are you now, Angela Corliss? What surprises do you have for me in this loop?

"Coffee." You close your eyes briefly, as if I've just said the magical word. Then you look at me and smile. "Someplace private. I don't want to be interrupted. Because you, Mr. Swan, are about to *talk*."

4

Science is a story to me. I could hear about science all day every day. Sit at someone's feet while they explain what they've wondered, what they tried, what they discovered.

This man Reggie Swan.

The stories he knows.

We sat in some kind of break room for what might have been three or four hours, me drinking coffee and munching on nuts and an apple and some chocolate they had on hand, interrupting him only when I needed more details, more explanation, but then letting him talk and talk and tell me.

Dear God, the things that man knows.

The things that man has done.

And even though I already saw it last night, my eyes kept going back to his left hand, that platinum ring on his wedding finger, as if this were a date we were on, not a lengthy interview between fellow scientists.

Although he wanted me to understand he is not a scientist. "Just a maker."

Just a maker. Spare me. A man who could invent what he has invented and has made the kind of advanced discoveries Reggie Swan has—that is citizen science at its core. He didn't need a physics degree like mine to do all he's done. That man's mind is superior to anyone's I've ever met.

As we rolled into hour four I could feel the day's strain. So much to learn and absorb. And just trying to get by on coffee and snacks.

"They make a reasonable dinner here," Reggie said. "Maybe we should take a break."

I smiled at that. But I was serious when I told him, "You're going to have to be the one to regulate this. Because I can honestly keep going all night. Right now I am an open vessel. I want everything you can possibly pour into it."

And then he did something I didn't expect. He started to reach for my hand, his fingers were almost to mine, when he abruptly pulled them back as if I'd scalded him. Fingers touching flame.

He got up from the plastic-topped table where we'd been sitting across from each other on standard-issue folding metal chairs. Same as in any university, any lab. Not meant for people to sink into and relax for too long, when there was important work to be done elsewhere.

I'll admit I was feeling pretty stiff by hour four, and I'd

taken only one restroom break when I couldn't hold my coffee anymore, but other than that, what I said was true. I was in it for the long haul. I could sit there all night.

Then, I'm embarrassed to say, I did my awkward best to find out. That almost-touching of my hand felt like a reason.

"You must … I mean, your wife must be waiting for you."

So blatant, so humiliatingly obvious. But it gave me the knowledge I needed.

Reggie smiled a sad smile. "She died, I'm very sorry to say."

"Oh." *Oh.* "I'm so sorry." And I was. And I wasn't.

"She was wonderful," Reggie said. "I miss her every day."

He seemed about to say more, but then he stopped himself.

"But we have our work, right?" he said. I nodded. I knew what he meant. A life of the mind is all-consuming. Except in those moments when it isn't.

I wasn't sure if I should ask, or if I actually wanted to know. But sometimes the mouth just moves on its own. "How long ago?"

"Ten years," Reggie said. He must have been in his early to mid-sixties then, close to my own age. He twisted the ring on his finger back and forth, what looked like absent-mindedly. But then he seemed to make up his mind about something.

He had to fight his finger a little to do it, but he got the ring free of it.

He pulled it off and tilted it to show me the engraving inside. Small, barely visible after however many years of wearing the ring against his skin, but I could see it once he pointed to it.

An A, underlined. <u>A</u>

"It was a joke," Reggie told me. "She put the ring on my finger and then told me about it later that night. It's the Bar A, like a brand." Reggie made a sizzling sound, like a brand against flesh. "I was hers, she was mine. I liked the idea so much, we took her ring back to the shop and had a Bar R engraved on that one." Reggie shrugged. He seemed embarrassed to share with a relative stranger something so intimate.

"What was her name?" I wasn't sure I wanted to keep talking about her, but the words just automatically kept coming.

Reggie stared at the ring. "Anne." He slipped the ring back on his wedding finger. Then he stood up. "We need to eat. Come on."

And this time when he held out his hand he didn't take it away. I let him guide me to my feet.

If I held on a split-second longer than I should have…

So be it.

5

"There you are." Kirsten Simmens finds us in the cafeteria dining on stuffed manicotti and grilled zucchini. She sits beside Angela. "How are you feeling?"

Angela holds up her empty fork. "Better." She points the tines at me. "I wish I could go back thirty years. I feel like my whole career could have been different."

I look down at my plate. I can't bear to meet her eyes. To say something so innocent when it is the crux of my whole life.

I wish I had met her, too. Married her. Had twenty more years with her than I did.

That we haven't been separated these past ten. Do I get to count those as married years? I was married to her in my heart, even if she never knew it. Or knew me.

I stand up and pick up my plate. I need a temporary escape. I can feel the heat on my face. I need to cool it down. Re-establish equilibrium.

"Need more?" I ask.

Angela shakes her head and spears another chunk of manicotti. I turn to Kirsten. "Anything?"

Kirsten looks at me strangely.

For a moment I can't unlock my gaze. It is as if she is holding me there.

Some electrical or gravitational force. Something out of my control.

I have known Kirsten Simmens for nearly thirty years now. Part of it is in a life she doesn't know. And she never knew me in my married years. That was a whole other lifetime.

But there is a resonance between our minds. A certain frequency she taught me about when we both lived on base with our extraterrestrial friends RayJay, Linus, and Mit.

It's been a long time since I have felt her mind locked onto mine.

"Second life?"

The fear of it snaps me free. How did she hear me when I tried so hard not to think it? Everything has to go as planned. We worked it out, you and me. I can't risk a single wrong move.

"Let it go," I warn Kirsten in my mind, and I walk away with my plate.

She doesn't follow me physically. She doesn't need to.

"Reggie—"

I quit walking. But I can't face her. *"Please."*

Then I can feel the memories flooding through my brain, and there is nothing I can do to stop them. The way

RayJay taught me to search the universe for the one my heart longed for. The moment I found Angela Corliss. The way I *knew*. Absolutely knew.

The same way RayJay taught me to navigate the universe. Locking on to my destination and instantly finding myself there. The thrilling and unexpected ease of it.

Angela was my destination. But there was no guarantee our life together would go on and on. Humans are fragile. Humans die. No matter how much they are loved.

But you are wise, sweetheart. Brilliant. Your mind operates at a level no one else's can.

And time is mutable. RayJay taught me that. Past, present, future, all of it happening at the same time in different slices, so that what you think hasn't happened yet already has, just on a different slice of your timeline.

You died. I watched you. It broke my heart to watch you.

But—and—we already had this other plan. You looped out of your old life into this second one. You never really died. No matter what my eyes thought I saw.

"Please," I beg Kirsten. *"She can't know. She doesn't want to know."*

I turn back and look at both of them. At you calmly polishing off your dinner, at Kirsten calmly gazing back at me.

To my relief, Kirsten just smiles.

She doesn't seem surprised by any of it.

"I've seen a lot of unbelievable things," she reminds me.

I watch her say something to Angela, then Kirsten gets up and comes walking toward me.

I can feel my heart panicking. I might have just ruined my chances. Things aren't unfolding the way they should be. We had everything so carefully planned out.

Not that I stuck to it all, letter for letter. Those times when I couldn't resist coming to see you, even for just a brief glance, a momentary interaction. I admit it, I haven't been pure about our plan. But it's a lot to ask of a man to stay away from the one he loves. I did my best. But knowing you were alive in my world was just too impossible to ignore. Maybe someone else could have kept to our strict no-contact rules, knowing the consequences if it didn't work. But over time, all the years without you, it turned out I couldn't do it.

And now I'm a stranger to you and you have no reason to trust me. You could leave here tomorrow and go on with your second life, and I would have to let you go. I can't interfere. You have to live it the way you are meant to live it. We both agreed on that.

And if we met again—when we met again—we would fall in love or we wouldn't. Although you were so sure you would. You told me so. Like a puzzle piece slipping into place.

Kirsten stands beside me now and speaks quietly out loud, rather than in my mind.

"You should tell her. She can take it. You have no idea what we just went through. She's strong and she's brave. Trust me, she'll want to know."

Kirsten lays a hand briefly on my shoulder, then walks on.

But not without a parting thought, mind to mind.

"Come on, Reggie, haven't you both lost enough time already?"

6

In my past you say you knew me. I don't remember. I've tried to. I try to picture it the way you've described it. But it's not there. That past is a blank.

But this present is here. This future is creating itself second by second, right in front of us.

You have a ring that fits me perfectly, even though my left ring finger is not a typical size. I fell off my bike when I was young and the bone never properly healed. But when you showed it to me—engraved with the **R**, the Bar R—and I slid it over the misaligned second joint, the ring settled perfectly into place as if it had always been there. I'm never taking it off.

It's just like you. Familiar, comfortable, right. The kind of man I would have wanted to be with in this life or any other. Loving, wise, and unbelievably smart. Resourceful and safe. The kind of man a lost and hungry kitten would come running to. The kind that extraterrestrials know they can trust their secrets to and can teach how to take the human race further.

The kind a physicist on the run who has to completely remake her life again would choose to be by her side. I choose you. Let's go forward and make something new.

My life is not what I expected it to be. Yours isn't, either. And here we are.

This age, this place, these experiences, this time.

Second life, third life, maybe more lives than I can count—it doesn't matter. I know what I know. It's here in the hearts of both of us. I believe we will find each other every time.

And for now, this particular present and this future, you are taking me to meet your friends and find out everything I want to know. And since I want to know everything, we might be gone a long time.

Although what is time once you learn to move backward and forward, just as distance means nothing once you understand the true secret to travel.

We leave tomorrow on a second honeymoon, this time out to the stars where you found your friends RayJay, Mit, and Linus, and where you learned from them how to find me the first time, and then how to find me again.

The heart has its own map, you told me. It knows exactly where to go.

Across galaxies, across time, across lives.

From now on I'm coming with you.

Next in the Dove Season Universe
EXPLORER

- Sharman Hix leads her first exploratory team out to unknown and uncharted planets filled with creatures no one has ever seen. Every new step forward is a risk. And those risks are more dangerous than any of them imagined.
- Biologist and alien hunter Julie Trident wants to help rather than harm. But her sympathetic heart exposes all of them to disaster.
- Hotshot pilot Arnie Camper never turns down the chance to test some new experimental aircraft. But flying on other planets is a whole other game.
- Kirsten Simmens can hear alien voices. What she hears this time leads her to dark places where no one else can follow.
- Pilot Frieda Wiles depends on her orderly, rational mind. But faced with the dangers of a bizarre new planet, is it time to rely on intuition instead?

A standalone collection in the Dove Season Universe. The universe if full of secrets. Only the explorers will discover what they are.

ABOUT THE AUTHOR

Robin Brande is an award-winning author, former trial attorney, black belt in martial arts, Reiki Master, and wilderness medic. Her outdoor adventures range from the Rocky Mountains to the Alps to Iceland.

She writes in multiple genres, including mystery, adventure, fantasy, science fiction, young adult, romance, and self-help.

For more information:
https://robinbrande.com/

For updates about upcoming installments of DOVE SEASON, along with previews and special discounts, subscribe to the Robin Brande newsletter: https://robinbrande.com/pages/subscribe.

MORE FROM ROBIN BRANDE

SHOW YOUR BOOK-LOVING STYLE!

AND SCIENCE LOVING, ART LOVING, DOG AND CAT LOVING, AND MORE...

Treat yourself to a soft, comfy, custom-made T-shirt designed by Robin Brande herself, inspired by her own books. You can see all of them at robinbrande.com/collections/t-shirts.

And here's a secret just for you: Use the discount code **READER10** at checkout to get **10% off any items in the store**. That means books, T-shirts, hoodies, mugs—whatever you'd like. Go ahead and treat yourself, book lover.

CERTIFIED
BOOK NERD
CERTIFIED
DOG NERD
CERTIFIED
SCIENCE NERD

books
every
day

Sleep enough
Eat enough

FIRST TWO RULES OF
Adventure
SLEEP ENOUGH
EAT ENOUGH

Retired psychology professor Dr. Winifred Parsons spent decades studying the human psyche as a scientist and academic. But she also explored it from another angle: Winnie Parsons is clairvoyant.

Now Winnie uses her psi talent to help clients resolve mysteries that are outside the reach of standard investigations.

The path to justice might be twisted, but Winnie always finds a way.

Life after death, miracle healings, communication with other species...

- *The Water Healers*: A nurse investigates rumors of miracle healers in Mexico.
- *A Drop of Sweat*: A clairvoyant secretly uses her skills to unravel the mystery of who destroyed a scientist's lab.
- *The Refugees*: A volunteer helps the refugees fleeing a planetary disaster.
- *The Bridge*: A grieving widow refuses to believe her husband is gone forever.
- *The Outpost Away from the World*: A scientist returns to the off-the-grid cabin of her childhood and discovers the mysterious secret to her survival.

The mountains can dish it out. But that doesn't mean you have to take it.

- *On Red Mountain*: A woman must survive alone in the mountains after her husband is struck by lightning.
- *The Rescue*: A mountain hermit and his dog race to avert a coming disaster—one that the dog senses before anyone else.
- *Home Deer*: A mountain widow takes matters into her own hands to protect the nearby woodland creatures.
- *The Gold Hunter*: An injured climber's only hope for survival is a stranger who won't give up.
- *Taken at Rustler Pass*: A teen girl fights to survive against the stranger who wants her dead.

High school senior and amateur physicist Audie Masters discovers a parallel universe—along with a parallel version of herself.

It's the adventure of a lifetime.

Now all she has to do is survive it.

Read all four books in the exciting, mind-bending PARALLELO-GRAM QUARTET. You'll never look at the universe or your own life the same way again.